This Book Has Been Gifted To:

_____

From A Bearer of Glad Tidings:

_____

Adah and The Great Seven

*An Allegory Tale on Politics
and the End of Taxes*

Damon M. White

Diana S. DesChamps

DesChamps Books
An imprint of DesChamps World Media

Story expanded as featured in the film Holy Galileo.

Other books by Damon White:
The Presence of The Path
The Inevitable Versus Destiny
The Meeting of Intuition
(Propt Presequence)
The Royalty, Peons, and the Martyr
The Monarch of Philosophy
The Grasshopper of Winter
The Mountains of Oceana
The Coming of the Praying Mantis
Equanomics
The Universal Wheel
Philosophical Fragments, Volume One

plus many others

ADAH AND THE GREAT SEVEN.
Copyright © 2016 by Damon M. White and Diana S. DesChamps.

www.damonwhite.com
www.holygalileo.com
www.twitter.com/holygalileo

DesChamps Books may be purchased for
educational, business,
or sales promotional use.
For more information please write:
Special Markets Department,

DesChamps World Media,

P.O. Box 1292, Dripping Springs, Texas, 78620, USA.

www.dcworldmedia.com

Designed by Diana Star

First DesChamps Books paperback edition published 2016

A CIP catalogue record for this book is available from the Library of Congress.

ISBN 978-1-365-13782-2

To all of those who won't get fooled again...

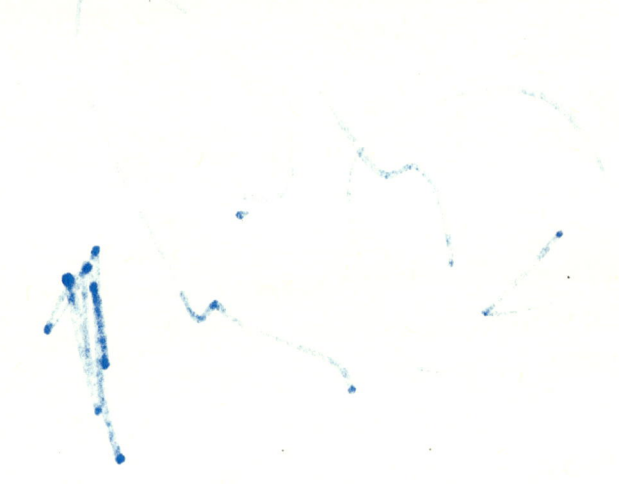

Authors' Note

This is the third version of this story. The first version is a rudimentary sketch released by Damon in 2012. A second version was enhanced by Diana and Damon in the film Holy Galileo. From that enhancement, Diana and Damon decided a definitive version had to be written in order to share the many layers involved in this story. 5-26-16

Introduction

Taxes!

The one constant obligation.
The most divisive burden ever conceived.
The one economic tabulation we are drilled into thinking we cannot possibly live without.

Until Now!

This book is written and can only be truly understood from the mindset that knows taxes and any of its derivative forms are the direct result of sinister minds concocting wealth inhibitors in conjunction with our own ignorance to be able to know and do better. In other words, no matter how well intentioned the usage of taxes, whether that be to redistribute the wealth or ensure the social welfare of the masses, continuing to use taxes to perform these functions, with the arrival of our new economic theory, is like using candles rather than light bulbs to illuminate New York City. Such can be done, but think of the fire hazard.

Every thought, principle, maxim and idea contained and relayed through this book is from a mindset which has embraced an economic system which said goodbye to taxation and the creation of money through a debtor process in order to welcome a much fuller and more enriching generator and distributor of wealth for the world.

BON VOYAGE!

Like a ship leaving a harbor belonging to an old world in order to sail to a new world, this book is your ticket to a new adventure beyond the stale and tired economic divisions based on a begrudging unity of taxation and debt.

Welcome aboard, let's get you oriented with the format of this ship.

This ship has many cabins for you to explore as we sail onward to the New World. We recommend you walk through the ship first before you spend too much time in any one cabin.

In Adah's story you will find a footnote after every couple of stanzas in a different language. Each footnote is a thought, idea, principle or maxim that supports and enhances the two stanzas. The translations are found in the Appendix. You can look up the translations as you read the story, yet, such might divert one's attention from the content of the story during the initial presentation. We suggest you read Adah's story in its entirety first, and then return for a rereading and a delving into each footnote.

One might actually find a certain footnote to mean more to them than anything else written in this book. Such might be one's cabin for the voyage.

Most of you will dine with us in the banquet hall with Adah at the head of the table imploring us to enjoy the feast as we put an end to taxes.

We call the feast, Equanomics, which is the title of the new economic foundation that shall emancipate us from the monetary tyranny of taxation.

Like any map which promises a New World, this book shall point us in the right direction. We have found that New World and invite you to come live with us there beyond taxes.

Let's Dig In and Set Sail!

Adah and The Great Seven

One's place is as much where one is as one is going.
Presently one is here reading this book to get to where one belongs in the New World.
Arriving is leaving.
Balancing these two places is where one finds harmony.
One cannot find harmony unless there is a potential for conflict between two or more things.
As you read this book, there is one question that will come to mind over and over again.
If I am here, and I am headed toward where this book is leading me,
then where is everyone else...
and more importantly,
where are they headed?

The Preface

The Eagle and The Wren

High above a tumultuous storm, a wren, miniature compared to the Eagles, the sole inhabitants of this elevation, out of breath, exclaimed,
"I'm not supposed to be here!"

The Eagle, a tad puzzled by the presence of a wren where only Eagles can fly, counseled,
"You are not supposed to be anywhere. You are either here or you are not. If you are here, then be here, and if you are not here, don't try to be here. Be where you are."

The wren emphatically declared,
"I am not meant to fly this high!"

The Eagle, amused by the wren's sense of displacement,
"Apparently your wings disagree with you."

The wren, shifting in spirit, enquired,
"What do I do here?"

The Eagle, sensing the wren's new-found comfort,
"What would you be doing down there right now?"

The wren confidently confessed,
"Cowering and hiding from the storm."

The Eagle laughed,
"Well, you obviously can't do that here, so you'll have to adapt."

The wren, curious for instruction,
"What do you do here?"

The Eagle laughed again,
"What you ought to be doing, enjoying the peaceful view."
The Eagle continued,
"As this is the best place to be in a storm, safely above it."

The wren felt an impulse of what she was supposed to be doing right now, and she didn't feel like enjoying the view. "How long have you Eagles known this is the best place to be in a storm?"

The Eagle responded with pride,
"Since we cannot remember not knowing."

The wren incredulously continued the interrogation,
"And yet you've never shared this with any of us below?"

The Eagle took umbrage at the semi-accusation,
"We most certainly have shared this truth with everyone below, but when faced with any truth from us, those below only listen to enforce their limitations, rather than appreciate the potential for so much more exhibited by us."

The wren understood and recalled her own disbelief at finding herself above the storm.
"I hear you now when I only listened before. We tell ourselves that the high places where the Eagles fly are not meant for us, due to our perceived deficiency... That the Eagles like to boast that they can go where none of us can, due to nothing more than being blessed by nature with a larger stature and wingspan... We mask our limitations by pretending we are braver than the Eagles because we face the storm below, while the Eagles only fly above never risking death by thunderbolt and high winds... We only do this mimicking the generations of birds before us..."

While the wren paused, the Eagle interjected,
"We only tell you of this place to let you know more of ourselves, not more of what you might be missing about yourself."

The wren as if waking from a short nap,
"Yes, I see, you were only being what Eagles are and we were only being what the birds below are. Perhaps it is time for us to do more than listen to each other, we must hear a new truth."

The wren darted toward the dark clouds.

The Eagle, surprised by the wren's sudden descent,
"Where are you going?!"

The wren hollered back,
"To tell the others that this is the best place to be in a storm!"

The Eagle, perplexed and alarmed,
"But it is storming, shouldn't you wait until the storm is over?"

The wren hollered again,
"During a storm is the best time to show those caught in a storm there is a place they can go to be above it, so no better time than now to save them from this storm!"
And off she disappeared into the dark, ominous clouds below.

The Eagle smiled and began to expect company.

For a whole two seconds.

The Eagle, admiring the wren's bravery knew he had to honor her by following her into the black, menacing clouds...
For the wren could instruct others on where to go, but the Eagle could carry them.

Part One

Same Ole Same Ole

1

**It is that time again,
when the birds elect
which group of birds
will govern them for a spell...
Hopes and apprehensions clash and collide
to mold the zeitgeist of the times...
The group of birds who lost the last election
are hoping to take over
from the presently reigning group of birds
who feel tentatively entitled
to maintain control...**

2

**There are two groups vying for the leadership...
The same two as always...
The Cardinals and the Blue Jays...
The Reds versus the Blues...
These labels versus those labels...
Empty promises versus vacant slogans...
This scam versus that sham...
Same ole same ole...**

Victors Willing Victory
German:
Sieger wird zum Sieg, Verlierer finden, einen Weg zu verlieren. Ein Wille zum Sieg schmiedet einen Weg zum Sieg, der Wille über irgendeiner Weise auszuüben. Verlieren ist eine Art und Weise über den Willen aufzugeben. Die Victor will die Verlierer, auf diese Weise vorzulegen.

3

**And there is one unsolvable issue,
one persistent problem,
which distresses everyone the most,
always has...
Supposedly always will...
Those Egg Snatching Snakes...**

4

**It doesn't matter which group leads them,
the unelected group opines
about tragic incidents until certain polls reflect
that Snatches are on the rise...
While the elected leadership group
uses stats and data to influence other polls
to show that Snatches are declining...**

The Eternal Problem
Chinese (Mandarin):

永恒的问题是唯一的永恒，因为掌权的几个关键人物保持可解决的问题，解决的每一个人，这是他们保持自己没有其他比他们负责维持和维护尚未成为亟待解决的问题的解决方案。因此，他们称之为永恒的问题，以抵御任何从实际上解决问题和暴露，主管领导人实际上存在的问题仍然不能解决的原因。

5

Back and forth the winning side proclaims a mandate
that the losing side will most certainly defy...
while the winning side is busy plugging,
the losing side is busy clogging,
invariably blocking any mojo toward a flow
necessary to truly solve the problem with the Snakes
(unknown to the voters is this secret: both sides have
mastered and enjoy being pluggers or cloggers);
Sometimes the Cardinals win,
Sometimes the Blue Jays win...
Nothing ever really changes,
So, actually, the Snakes always win!

6

That is, until on this day,
a new champion would rise;
not from the Cardinals,
not from the Blue Jays,
and definitely not from the Snakes.
No, a new champion would rise
from the Owls.

Great Deception Essence
Japanese:
本当の問題が解決するまで、選挙は勝つ-
いくつかし、多くの失う失います。選挙に勝利し、勝者は勝ちます。彼らは大衆に苦しむ必要があります直接現実の問題を解決できていないため受賞者の障害になるので敗者は勝ちます。これらのいくつかの受賞者のみ問題に直面しないこれら直接の固まりのないので。しかし、大衆を失う失うため問題で立ち往生のまま選挙を勝に関係なく威圧的な問題を軽減する誰も失います。とき勝利を失う失うにつながる、このような偉大な詐欺の本質です。

7

This young hooter from an artistic and philosophical clan of
Owls had imagined a daring and strategic plan
on enforcing the futile Snake snatching ban...
Offering no proof or credentials
on how such can be done
the young hooter only
offered an epiphany, a call to greatness,
and some freedom fun.

8

The young hooter revealed defiantly,
"Yeah, the Cardinals tell us our only hope is the Hawks
and the protection they offer,
which does cost us dearly,
cause ya know, freedom isn't free, right?
Well, despite the best efforts of the Hawks
to keep the Snakes out
they still find a way to sneak in and snatch away..."

Prove By Improvement
Russian:
Доказательство не подтверждает теорему, доказательство подтверждает, что теорема не нуждается в доказательствах.

Доказывая это так не будет делать это не так, это будет просто показать, что это было так еще до того, один пытался доказать, что это было так.

Слишком много усилий помещается в это доказать и / или что, и не достаточно усилий направлены на улучшение этого и / или что.

Будь Улучшитель , а не просто Доказывающий .

9

The young hooter continued,
"And the Blue Jays tell us that our only hope
is in trusting the treaties that the doves make with the Snakes.
Yet, whatever the allotment of eggs allocated to the Snakes
through these one-sided agreements,
such never, ever satisfies their greed...
And they always demand a tad more
than we were supposedly ever willing to give...
So we increase the allotment each and every time."

10

"Every time we elect either group,
whether this be the Cardinals
who promise strength through action,
or the Blue Jays,
who promise power through ideas,
we expect them to do something
they simply are not capable of doing,
because if they did,
their political groupings would be no more..."

Be More Than Peace
Greek:
Σε έναν κόσμο διαιρεμένη, ο στρατός και οι διπλωμάτες εργαστεί χέρι με χέρι να διατηρήσει τη διαίρεση. Οι διπλωμάτες μεσολαβήσει μια συνθήκη ειρήνης που είναι στη συνέχεια, σπασμένα, επομένως υπαγόρευσαν στους στρατιωτικούς να πάει στον πόλεμο μέχρι οι διπλωμάτες πάρετε μαζί και πάλι να σας συστήσει μια άλλη συνθήκη ειρήνης, η οποία στη συνέχεια θα σπάσει. Η σιωπηλή αλήθεια αυτό δεν τελειώνει ποτέ, φαύλος κύκλος είναι ότι οι κοινωνίες μας πάει έσπασε χωρίς την αποτίμηση προήλθε από τον πόλεμο. Ως εκ τούτου, μια συνθήκη ειρήνης συμπροσαρμοσμένων είναι στην πραγματικότητα μια δήλωση ότι οι δύο κοινωνίες έχουν χρεοκοπήσει και πόλεμο για να αποκτήσουν ξανά αξία. Πραγματική ειρήνη είναι μόνο μια πραγματική αξία όταν πρόκειται για ένα δεδομένο, δεν είναι μια αιτία. Ώστε να είναι περισσότερο από την ειρήνη... Περισσότερα από ειρηνική, έτσι ώστε η ειρήνη και being ήσυχος είναι o givens των ενεργειών σας, δεν είναι η αιτία. Τότε και μόνο τότε θα μπορείτε να δείτε το τέλος του την ανάγκη για πόλεμο.

11

The young hooter then delivered a type of promise
unheard before any election,
"I promise that I'm going to do
what needs to be done BEFORE the election...
Before we vote again and congratulate ourselves
that we at least voted for the best promissor
of the same ole same ole,
whose begging for power to win the election
is only matched by their pleading for understanding
and even sympathy they were just as powerless
to do anything after the election as they were before."

12

"And I am going to do it in order to bring out
the best from each side to the point
they will question themselves on why they
were ever divided between the Reds and the Blues
in the first place to solve a problem
which required them to be
neither Red nor Blue.
Who is with me?"

Same Ole Same Ole
Italian:
Ci sono tre emozioni forti per ogni elettore. Sei felice il vostro candidato ha vinto. Tu sei ancora più felice l'altro candidato ha perso. Alla fine si convivere con un rimpianto per tutta la vita che tu abbia mai votato per il candidato. Poi si arriva a ridere di quelli che ti dicono che il loro ultimo candidato rompere questo ciclo di melanconia elettori follia.

13

Now, the elders of all the Owl Clans
recognized the dangerous precedent
being set by the young hooter.
So, being more concerned about their reputation
for being smarter than any emotion,
for being objective over any bias,
for being uniform without being misinformed,
than for the welfare of this young hooter,
thwarted this effort to call
upon volunteers from the start...

14

They instructed that no other Owl participate
in any scheme this young hooter
had wantonly dreamed...
Or they would suffer the fate
of the scurrilous Pigeons
or felonious Seagulls
(Either be with the Pigeons
forced to live in polluted cities
or join the Seagulls lost by the Sea)...
SABOTAGE!
And they figured... Wrongly...
That would be the end
to this foolishness...

Changing By Not Changing
French:
Quand les gens agissent différemment mais pense la même chose, ils ont rien fait plus que changer eux-mêmes et pas le monde. Lorsque les personnes agissent de la même chose mais pensent différemment, puis ils ont changé le monde malgré eux. Pour vraiment faire les deux, on doit agir et penser différemment... Changer soi-même n'est pas suffisant, et changer le monde ne suffit pas... Le processus comprend un et est également au-delà de l'un en même temps...

15

The elders of the Owl Clan smugly thought
they had crashed and burned
the young hooter's whimsical phantasm
of a pursuit of greatness.
The young hooter fully expected this overreaction,
and pretended that the elders had stopped this effort
so the necessary work would be done unencumbered
by their foolish attempts at sabotage...

16

There was no farewell party...
The Owl elders figured the young hooter
would be gone for good
but the young hooter knew
it wasn't for good...
It was for the best for all involved
because this young Snowy Owl would return
with something they truly wanted
but they didn't want to obtain it
the only way it could be done.
So, the young hooter flew far away
to the domain of the Eagles
to ask them for a huge favor...

Fear-Mongering Derelicts
Polish:
Ci, którzy próbują wyłączyć wyobraźnię są jak mieszkaniec ziemi opowiadał marynarza, że nie powinni ustawić żagiel wzdłuż równika od Afryki do Ameryki Południowej, ponieważ nie są niebezpieczne góry lodowe w morzu. Marynarz odpowiada potwierdzeniem niebezpieczeństwa "Tak, istnieją góry lodowe w morzu, ale są one nigdzie w pobliżu, gdzie chcemy być. I to, że nie będą mogli zobaczyć aż na pokład mojego statku i ustawić popłynąć ze mną. " Doświadczenie przebija mądrość tylko wtedy, gdy jest niewłaściwie mądrości, dzięki czemu jest nierozsądne, aby być mądrym.

Part 2:

Assembling the Z Team

17

Normally, the Eagles, who almost always soar
far above the riff-raffing, rant-raving fray below them,
would have ignored the young hooter...
And would have declined any requests
from those who cannot fly above the storm.
They anticipated that the young hooter's request
would be about the Snakes.
For every request asked of the Eagles
by the lower form of birds, was always about the Snakes,
as if the Eagles had no other purpose than
to kill Snakes for the rest of the birds.
They fully expected to decline this request.

18

Yet, this young hooter was different than all the rest.
When every Eagle resoundingly said "No!" to the young
hooter's request, the young hooter countered,
"I would be scared too, if I was only an Eagle like you,
to do what I'm now asking of you."
The Eagles' feathers began to ruffle and a kerfuffling
could be heard murmuring throughout the convocation.
"For it has been too long since any of us have seen you
engaged in any real battle with the Snakes.
By declining to come with me now,
doubts will begin on which group of birds are actually
the bravest, with us Owls overtaking your top spot."
With the honor of their pride on the line,
the Eagles accepted the young hooter's request.

Imagination Is The Greatest Magic
Hungarian:
Minden valóság folytatása mindenki fantáziáját. Azok, akik nem elképzelni az életet, nem vesznek részt teljes körűen az életben. A megfigyelők, magyaráz, panaszosokat, rögzítők és oly sok más hozzá kevés az élet és a halál ... megpróbálják leállítani a képzelet olyan életnek nincs lövés megváltoztatni őket, és úgy érzi, él ... az élet folyamatosan kreatív ... haldokló nem ...

19

**With the support and endorsement of the Eagles,
the young hooter turned to the exiled ones,
the falcons, allegedly the murderers of fellow birds,
and offered them an enticing bargain
that could cost them the ultimate price
but offer full redemption and reconciliation...**

20

**The young hooter appealed to the
falcons' desire to be accepted and respected
knowing they feel equal to the Hawks
who feel equal to the Eagles
even if they are being treated as less than a grackle.
"Not only will your banishment be lifted
if you participate and perform this well,
you will be lauded as heroes..."**

Bargaining For A Bargain
Dutch:
Echte koopjes zijn gemaakt wanneer beide kanten hefboom om de andere kant te overtuigen. Het is net als de wip op de speelplaats, de koop niet volledig kan worden gemaakt totdat beide kanten leren elkaar te verheffen in een motie waarin momentum biedt voor beide partijen. Een koopje dat slechts verheft ene kant is een zwendel. En oplichting kan zijn door een opgetild of degene vallen op de bodem.

21

The falcons responded in disbelief,
"The Hawks made us their enemy
just to kill us for sport,
since the Crows control the media,
any effort of self-defense by us is called an attack,
and the Doves have smeared our name
leading to our banishment,
therefore we get scapegoated
by the Blue Jays and Cardinals!"

22

"Yes, yes, yes..." soothed the young hooter,
"Your bad reputation is a political calculation,
and the target on your back is a military strategem.
Without a proper voice and proper defense,
you are easy prey and a weak enemy
for the status quo to abuse, yet,
if you do this for me,
your actions will speak louder
than their slanderous words
and you'll be honored above
any of our staunchest allies."

Things As Each Are
Czech:
Co mnozí perspektiva hovor je zpravidla rozpis toho, co dělá něco pro ně, nebo to, co se přece jen něco je, a obvykle na úkor druhého. Kompletní perspektiva ukazuje, jak a využívá odlišnosti obou směrem k plnosti reality. Co se něco dělá a co něco nejsou stejné a nabízejí různé interpretace reality, a to je jen o tom, které aspekty obou odlišných výkladů, jako je právě proto, že něco je něco, co neznamená, že něco udělal něco, co vychází z toho, co to je , a jen proto, že něco udělal něco neznamená, že je něco jen proto, že to udělal. Být schopen rozlišit mezi tím, co něco, co je a co dělá něco, co je klíčem k odrážející plnost reality prostřednictvím svého pohledu.

23

After much hem-hawing and debate
the falcons finally agreed on one point.
They would like nothing better
than to make the Hawks honor them for their bravery,
and to make the Doves be held accountable
for misrepresenting the falcons' value...
And most of all to show what do-nothings
the Cardinals and the Blue Jays really are.
Henceforth, the young hooter's plan was named
by the falcons as operation Snake Farmer Charmer!

24

With the majestic Eagles and
the feisty falcons on board,
the young hooter knew
that the biggest challenge was up ahead
in the exotic land of disenchantment
with the obstinate Ostriches!

Phonetic Fallacies
Fun with English Sound Similarities:

Reed naught, here! Lien clothes. Tails sail. Dew rite. Sore hi. Won wood bee grate. Hour sun maid reign, sew aisle four bare. Weight two sea doe till nun no blew ore read. Heel meat yew wear Taxus our knot. Lead buy lite threw whiled knight. Isle prays know wholly lyre, borne bowled. Thyme scent too he'd holey col. Vein perish soled cowered spill. Eye cents ewe new. Taut weather wheel lye oar dye, sow cher you're holy lessen. Stair wile wee berry yore crewed thrown.

25

**The Ostriches' reaction to
Operation Snake Farmer Charmer
was typical of a group who
shunned any conflict or fray...
"Are you insane or just plain crazy?"
The Ostriches felt that the
mere asking of the young hooter's sanity
would intimidate and run the young hooter off.**

26

**The young hooter surprised them by agreeing to both.
"Of course I'm insane, who would ever dare
challenge the Great Seven directly as I propose we do?
And of course I'm just plain crazy, I have to be,
cause I fully expect this plan to work.
Yet what is more insane and crazy,
is to hear this plan and not act on it
when one is vital and fully capable
of helping make it successful,
and free themselves and all birds
from the tyranny of the Great Seven
once and for all."**

True Insanity
Portuguese:
Insanidade é saber a coisa certa a fazer, e que você está destinado a fazê-lo, e fazê-lo irá resultar em alguma coisa boa acontecendo para você, mas você é incapaz de agir sobre o que você sabe. Nós concebeu o conceito de escolha para esconder nossa insanidade.

27

**The Great Seven
were the Seven Great Python Leaders
of the Snake Kingdom.
No birds have ever interacted with the Great Seven
and come away alive other than the Eagles,
valiant and expertly skilled enough
to kill any Snake, even the Great Seven,
which is the real reason the Great Seven
burrow deep underground with
the natives of the cavern, the Bats,
and the pets of the court, the Peacocks.**

28

**Yes, the Ostriches agreed among themselves
that without them the plan would not work,
yet they began to feel crazy enough
that it might work with their help
and even worse or perhaps better
they felt insane enough to want to do it
even though if the plan failed
they would be the arch enemy
of the Seven Great Pythons forever...
So they joined in the cause
because it kinda felt good
to be crazy and insane for once.**

God's Ignorance
Hindi:

भगवान तो भगवान जानता था कि भगवान के निर्माण से पहले भगवान से पूछा था। और भगवान ने उत्तर दिया, "निर्माण तक वहाँ था भगवान के लिए कोई ज़रूरत नहीं और इसलिए अपने आप को भगवान के रूप में पता करने के लिए मेरे लिए कोई ज़रूरत नहीं." भगवान से तब पूछा था 'यदि आप केवल बनाए जाने के बाद भगवान बन गया, जो और क्या आप निर्माण से पहले थे?' भगवान हँसे और कहा, "इससे पहले कि आप पता था कि तुम मेरे थे मैं आप था."

Part Three:

Entering Is Exiting

29

So, to the surprise of both the Eagles and the Hawks
the young hooter had pulled off
what many would have considered a minor miracle
getting the Ostriches to pull their heads
out of the ground and volunteer
for this dangerous act of rebellion
because the Ostriches had more allegiances
with roaming land mammals
than they did with birds of flight.

30

Now came the time for the Big Showdown!
The atmosphere electrified
as the young hooter and the caravan
entered the sacred den of the Great Seven...
Since no bird had entered the Snake den
for Ages beyond a time anyone could remember,
the Snakes were more amused than cautious
by this radical lunatic move by the young hooter.

Courage Is Leadership
Norwegian:
Mot er ikke bare å gjøre det man frykter, det er å være fet.

Swedish:
Modet inte gör vad alla fruktar måste göras, det är att vara modig.

Finnish:
Rohkeus on saada jokainen tarpeen tehdä, mitä he pelkäävät on tehtävä.

31

Amusement quickly turned to exasperation
while the young hooter pranced and preened
about some new era of cooperation
between the birds and the Snakes.
The Great Seven remained staunchly unimpressed,
until they noticed the young hooter's cargo...

32

The cargo that the young hooter had brought were
21 of the biggest, freshest, most delicious looking
Ostrich eggs that the Great Seven had ever seen...
They were now intensely impressed...
And decided to let the young hooter live
long enough to see them enjoy these eggs.

Everything Is, Nothing Is
Korean:
당신이 그들에 게 하지 않았다 또는 도둑 질 이라고, 그들과 함께 그것을 공유 하는 경우 어떤 사람 으로부터 뭔가 받을 수 없다. 당신이 그것을 걸릴 하지 않습니다 또는 당신에 게 서 그것을 공유 하는 사람에 게 뭔가 드릴 수 없습니다. 그는 침입. 촬영 하거나 당신이 나 다른 사람에 의해 주어진 수 없는 뭔가 공유할 수 없습니다. 그 라고 속이 고. 우주 촬영, 주어진 하거나 우리에 대 한 우리 중에 의해 우리와 함께 공유 수... 우리는 우주를 복용 하 고, 공유를 넘어...입니다.

33

The young hooter cashed in on the moment,
"As you can clearly see, I came bearing glorious gifts.
We birds know how difficult it is for you
Snakes to snatch Ostrich eggs.
Not only is it dangerous for you
even to approach the nest of an Ostrich,
due to their powerful legs, even if you
swallowed an egg you are haplessly immobile
for them to stomp your guts out.
I bring more than gifts though, I bring also a bargain..."

34

The Great Seven nodded in agreement,
because they were once led by a King,
a Black Mamba,
until he suffered the gut-stomping fate
by the Ostrich named Orion,
who also later died because their fellow leader
continued biting its poisonous
death grip on Orion's neck,
even after his body was separated from his head.
The Great Seven slowly slid down
from their perch toward the eggs.

Impossibility Is Real
Slovak:
Niekedy je nemožné, je to, čo to slovo vlastne znamená, nie je možné. Ak nie je nič, čo je v skutočnosti nemožné, potom je úlohou nie je obrátiť nemožné, aby to možné, úlohou je nájsť to, čo je v skutočnosti nemožné.

35

"My Bargain is this, I will supply you
with an endless surplus of Ostrich eggs directly to you
if you will call off egg snatches in my land..."
Shy Star the Copperhead, attorney for the Great Seven
incredulously asked "What's in it for the Ostriches?"
The young hooter snapped back
"False hopes and broken dreams
all due to a sinister scheme,
something this bunch knows all too well."
And the Snakes had a belly full of laughs.

36

Even though the Snakes were now humored
by the Snaketonion quality of this young hooter,
amid all the bellowing and chuckling there was also a distinct
grunt of disapproval that they would be asked
to participate in and honor any bargain by the birds.
Yes, their end of the bargain was tantalizing,
the Ostrich eggs were the biggest,
tastiest and most satisfying,
and also they were damn near suicidal to snatch.
But snatching eggs was
a Snake's divine right everywhere,
no bargain was worth prohibiting a divine right.

Devil Defying Us
Turkish:
Şeytan bir kez kendim ve insanlık arasındaki sorun diğer grup akıl yoluyla Tanrı'ya meydan okuyan ise bizden biri ilkesine Tanrı'yı meydan okuyan o "dedi. Bizden biri bizim meydan okuyan firma standları, diğer grup arama yaparken ve herhangi bir görünüş tutunur neden Tanrı'ya meydan okumaya. İnsanlık benden nefret ediyor, onlar asla mükemmellik temsil çünkü. onlar beni öldürdü bile, Tanrı benim mükemmel meydan okuma hala sonsuza insanlığı uğrak olacaktır. " İnsanlık "Biz Allah'ı seviyorum, ve Allah bizi seviyor.", Cevap . Beni ben Tanrı olduğumu sanmıyorum Allah her zaman meydan için tüm hiçe sayarak en kibar şekilde ben de Tanrı'yı seviyorum, gerekli olduğunda; Şeytan meydan benim en sevdiğim biçimlerinden biri aşktır ", diye terslendi . " Tanrı'yı meydan okumaya nasıl gerçek bir tartışma için, onlar Allah değildi davranarak durdu Yani her ne zaman Şeytan geri gelmek için insanlığı talimat verdi.

The Great Seven snorted a deadly threat,
"Foolishly brave of you to enter here,
yet, we can agree to this deal and then demand the
deliverer of the Eggs become our dessert...
Being foolish or brave depends on whether
we agree to this deal or not and either
we make you and your entourage our dessert or we set you free."
A member of the entourage turned to look at a disappearing exit.
"Because you see that supposed looming shadow behind you
is actually many bats closing off your escape."

The young hooter expected such treachery from the Snakes.
"Yes, indeed, if you agreed to the deal and ate us,
our martyrdom would be a worthy sacrifice.
And even if you do not agree to the deal,
the risk was also worth showing the bird kingdom
that the Snakes could never be trusted.
One important detail not to overlook
since we are laying down our cards now,
that black cloud which followed me here and hovers above the den,
that is actually a convocation of proud, strong Eagles..."
The bats parted to show the legion of Eagles
which did send a shudder through the Great Seven
at the sight of their arch enemy.

The Opposite Of Opposite Is Another Opposite
Arabic:

غياب النور ليس الظلام، للضوء والظلام نوعان من طرفي الطيف نفسه. غياب الضوء يعني عدم وجود هذا الطيف التي تشمل أيضا غياب تلك الظلمة. على سبيل المثال، الضوء والظلام هي النشاط متبادل المعالين. يمكن أن يكون هناك أي ليلة من دون الشمس وعلى الجانب الآخر من العالم. هناك ما هو إذا كان هناك أي ضوء أو الظلام، كأن لا شيء يمكن أن ينظر إليها أو الغيب؟ الجواب في السؤال. أهلا وسهلا بك إلى لا شيء. لا شيء، إذا كان حقا لا شيء ولا حتى الظلام، لأنه حتى الظلام شيء. لا شيء يمكن أن يكون معروفا، لا شيء يمكن أن يكون غير معروف. لذلك أقول لكم لا يعرفون شيئا لا يعني شيئا غير معروف لك. غياب كل شيء لا شيء، حتى لعدم وجود شيء. ليس هناك ما هو وليس أي شيء.

39

The young hooter then delivered a deadly threat
"If I don't come out unharmed in due time,
those battle-ready Eagles,
normally above such skirmishes,
will cut off your supply chain,
until you are desperate enough and
forced out of this den due to your hunger.
Then those Eagles will pounce on you
when you must hunt
and carry you off to the Sea..."

40

The Snakes bellowed, "The bats would protect us!"
The young hooter sternly declared,
"We both know that the bats only respect and serve strength.
You being famished and weak would
shift their servitude to the Eagles,
and you would die from a million bat bites,
rather than the clutches of a hundred talons."
The Great Seven shrugged and
returned their focus to the Eggs,
"We agree to your terms, you will see another day,
so now let us each feast on an Egg tripledecker..."

Being Strong Assimilates
Albanian:
Të jesh i fortë është në gjendje të përballoj një forcë të trazuar. Kjo nuk do të thotë fshehur prej saj, drejtimin prej tij, ose duke e lejuar atë për të lëvizur ju në asnjë mënyrë. Një duhet të qëndrojmë të fortë me të në mënyrë që të tregojë forcën e dikujt. Përfundimisht një tames këtë forcë, dhe përdor atë për të bërë veten dhe të tjerët më të fortë.

41

"Feast Away!"
The young hooter exclaimed,
who was not fooled by the conciliatory
words of the Great Seven
for their arrogant demeanor gave them away, because,
Snakes, being Snakes, never kept any bargain in good faith.

42

So, when one makes a bargain with one
who never keeps a bargain
and still expects the bargain to be kept, such is folly,
and nothing more than an exhibition of ignorance and vanity.
If this was what the young hooter was doing
with the bargain and the Great Seven,
the leaders of the Owl Clan would have
been correct not to back such foolishness.
Yet, when one makes a bargain knowing
that the other side will not keep it,
such is the perfect opportunity to unleash a strategic
subversion upon the will of the bargain breakers...
The young hooter smiled as the
Great Seven devoured egg after egg...
Freedom was at hand.

One Can Honestly Lie
Hebrew:

קסם שנסך הוא פעולה כנה של שקר שאם תתקבלו יהיה לפקפק עניישה על תם למטרה הבלעדית של לתמרן אותם וכל מי מתייחס איתם לעשות מה מי מפתה אומר שהם חייבים לעשות כדי להרים פסק דין זה (קסם שנסך) ולתמוך שקר.קסם שנסך הוא פעולה של הונאה, ואילו כפירה היא רעיון של טעייה. ההבדל בין קסם שנסך ו כפירה הוא כפירה מהווה זרז פרדיגמה שלמה של הונאה, בעוד קסם שנסך מבקש להוסיף גוון וגוון של טעייה על פרדיגמה קיימת. קסם שנסך הוא סימפטום של כפירה. אנשים להונות אנשים שהם מחויבים כפירה.

43

After all 21 of the Ostrich Eggs had been swallowed,
three a piece for each of the Great Seven,
they were filled and stretched out euphorically,
yet, also vulnerably, if the young hooter had planned
an assassin-like attack, this would have been the time.
The young hooter made no such move.
The Great Seven felt safe and secure
to relish in the crushing of the Eggs.

44

"Ah, yes!" the young hooter exclaimed with maniacal glee.
"You can surely feel that I brought you eggs
with hatchlings moments away from bursting forth,
savor their mature desperation..."
Knowing this the Great Seven took delight
in the cracking of the shells as they slowly
and with tender care
constricted upon the helpless hatchlings...

Meanwhile, many miles away the Blue Jays and Cardinals
were in a heated debate over who could do less
but promise more than the other
when it came to those Egg-Snatching Snakes...

Be Happy Now, Celebrate Later
Swahili:

Furaha ni wakati moja ni sawa na kile sasa kinachotokea. Ili kubaki na furaha moja lazima sasa na kile kinachotokea umoja. ... Furaha ni hisia ya kushinda. Ili kusherehekea kikamilifu, furaha ni moyo wako kuruhusu unajua wewe ni kushinda. Sherehe ni akili yako kuruhusu unajua umefanya alishinda. Ili kusherehekea ni umoja kufurahia kile kilichotokea ... Mtu anaweza kuwa na furaha moja ni kushinda, lakini kusiwe na sherehe mpaka kuna ushindi.

Part Four:

Outsnaking the Snakes...

45
Triumphant, the Great Seven began to slowly
slide toward the young hooter
and the unwelcome entourage
to top off this banquet with
a tastier bit of fowl morsel called foolish arrogance...
The young hooter pointed to the sky
full of Eagles to which
the Great Seven ignored
like one does any bluff--
except the young hooter did not seem
to mind this bluff being called...
"Threatening Us will not save you,
but, you were doomed anyway."
The Great Seven laughed up
a few bits of egg shell...

46
The young hooter did not wince,
but puffed up instead...
"I most assuredly did not threaten you
with the Eagles, that was just a distraction
to ensure I could watch my real threat unfold."
The Snakes were undeterred.
"Watch as we devour your comrades fir--"
Suddenly, each snake felt a sharp pain,
too sharp for hatchlings to inflict...
The pains quickened,
becoming sharper with each constriction,
for, the Great Seven could not stop themselves
from gorging on the Eggs
even in severe pain...
To no avail, the Great Seven
tried to vomit up this supposed delicacy...
Too late, the Great Seven felt more than pain,
they began to feel real damage... And fear...

The Advantage of Disadvantage
Thai:
จุดอ่อนของความได้เปรียบใด ๆ
ในการเปิดเผยความอ่อนแอของคนที่มีความได้เปรียบใน
การเป็นผู้หนึ่งที่ไม่ได้มีความได้เปรียบเพราะได้เปรียบเผย
ให้เห็นจุดอ่อนในพวกเขา
ผู้ด้อยโอกาสอย่างใดอย่างหนึ่งแล้วจะต้องพบกับความใหม่ที่จะเอาชนะหนึ่งได้เปรียบที่ได้เปรียบอย่างใดอย่างหนึ่ง
จะไม่สามารถที่จะหาเพราะพวกเขาไม่ได้ถูกผลักไปยังพบ
ว่ามันเป็นเพราะพวกเขาไม่ได้ด้อยโอกาส
ความแข็งแรงหนึ่งได้เปรียบมาจากการมีข้อได้เปรียบในขณะที่ความแรงของคนด้อยโอกาสมาจากที่ไม่รู้จัก;
ความคิดสร้างสรรค์เป็นข้อได้เปรียบที่แข็งแกร่งในการต่อ
สู้ใด ๆ
ดังนั้นผู้ด้อยโอกาสคนเดียวที่ยังคงด้อยโอกาสหากพวกเขาล้มเหลวในการใช้ประโยชน์จากข้อได้เปรียบที่แข็งแกร่ง
และความคิดสร้างสรรค์

47

The Great Seven garbled one last exclamation,
for they were puzzled at what was happening to them,
yet, not by the method,
they recognized one who had outdone them
by being even more conniving than them...
"What have you done?
Those eggs were tainted,
you have out-snaked us snakes...
what about our bargain?"
The words sounded as futile
as the Great Seven now found breathing...

48

Since the beginning of their reign,
there have been many prophecies
made by various groups of birds
on how the Great Seven would perish.
Most were bird droppings... Only a few have merit...
Like those told by the Pelicans, the Vultures,
and the late, great Auks...
The Great Seven had taken great lengths
to thwart any and all of these prophecies...
And they had been and were still successful,
because what was now happening to them
could not be found in any prophecy...
This had come from the deadliest source of all,
the future masked as the present...

Wanting Without Need
Indonesian:

Ketika kita mendapatkan apa yang kita paling ingin, namun, kita tidak murni hatinya mengapa kita membutuhkannya, apa yang dimaksudkan untuk terjadi tidak terjadi karena sumber kemurnian penting disediakan oleh alam semesta bukan ... Kemurnian adalah apa yang dimaksudkan untuk diungkapkan, dan jika salah satu tidak memberikan kemurnian dari hati sendiri, alam semesta akan memberikan kemurnian yang satu gagal untuk menunjukkan untuk mengajar satu untuk menjadi murni dengan kebutuhan seseorang untuk apa yang paling ingin; Sayangnya, beberapa diajarkan pelajaran ini sulit untuk kematian mereka ... Oleh karena itu menjadi contoh bagi yang lain ketika seseorang gagal untuk belajar pelajaran keras yang ingin tanpa murni perlu mirip dengan menjadi haus dan mengabaikan salah satu yang memuaskan dahaga tersebut dengan minum dari sumur beracun.

49

No one had foreseen this... Not even the most gifted
from the Prophetic Realms...
Therefore, the Great Seven had no chance to stop it...
The Great Seven thought in Unison for the Last Time,
Such is the only way for the future to be the future,
and not just a continuation of the past...
*Futurum pertinet ad eos tantum... The Non amet
Praeteritum... Ave... Future Nobis fiunt recentium...*
(The Future Only Belongs to Those
Not Owned by the Past... Hail to the Future...
The Past and Us Are Done.)

50

"Oh", said the young hooter, "I made a bargain alright,
and it included the demise of all of you,
which appears to be happening right about now..."
The Great Seven writhed with severe convulsions,
blood spurting from their necks,
splattering the young hooter,
soon to be nicknamed,
The Crimson Crusader.
The Great Seven shook in shock
at what they saw pecking
through their wounds...
The young hooter marveled
at the expected and
unexpected young fledglings...

Be A Futurian
Romanian:
Ei spun că cei care nu învață din trecut, sunt sortite să-l repet ... dar eu spun, cei care învață doar din trecut, de asemenea, sortită Se repetă ... Unul Ori trăiește istorie sau Predă Istoria ... devine un exemplu viu al unui istoric și cel mai bine la doar o altă parte a istoriei ... Numai cei care știu și de a face ceea ce Istoria nu poate învăța cu adevărat trăiesc pe dincolo de istorie, ele sunt cele ale viitorului ...

51

Several young falcons,
fearless and energetic,
once hidden in the Giant Ostrich Eggs
as supposed helpless hatchlings,
were now bursting forth
from the Great Seven
like mighty avengers...

52

As their pecks separated the Great Seven Heads
from their Giant Python Bodies,
the falcons screeched what would reverberate
throughout the Snake Kingdom...
And All Kingdoms,
"Geronimo, Mother Fuckers,
the Great Seven are no more!"

The Greatest Deception
Haitian Creole:

Desepsyon nan pi gran se yon avètisman pwofetik ki desepsyon lan pi gran se toujou ap vini yo nan lòd yo twonpe moun ap tann pou yon gwo desepsyon vini nan kwè yo ke yo pa te deja te twonpe tèt nou pa desepsyon nan pi gran.
*- Soti nan liv **la inevitab la kont destine***

PART FIVE:

A New Era!

53

Just before the murkiness of death overtook their eyes...
And the Great Seven's heads bounced off the floor...
One could see a wily smirk curl up on their faces
in recognition of the young hooter's deviousness.
The giant Eagles flew in
unimpeded through the bats who now
scattered to pay homage to the new strength
by screeching thunderous applause as the Eagles
snatched the Great Snatchers' heads
and set out to fly the lengths of the World
to show the Great Seven were long gone...

54

The Eagles proclaimed, "Long live this day of freedom
from the tyranny of the Great Seven!
Never again shall any bird live in fear of any Snake!"
As the world celebrated the demise of the Snakes' overlordship,
The Blue Jays and Cardinals scrambled for and poached at a way
to politically spin this world changing event in their favor, because
when you boil it down to their one and only motivation, garnering
undeserving votes has no shame whenever substance is lacking.
Soon propaganda began making the rounds that inferred and
implied that the Blue Jays or the Cardinals were somehow
instrumental in the taking down of the Great Seven.
Both sides claimed the young hooter belonged to them.

Revolve or Advance
Spanish:
En general, la llamada para el cambio de las masas se deriva de un estado de aburrimiento de los que en el escenario. Y por lo general cuando los actores son reemplazadas y el guión se rehashed prometer la misma recompensa no se puede entregar la alegría de masas y aplauden la vieja demostración hizo de nuevo una vez más. El asentamiento de equivalencia sobre la excelencia es la clave a la esclavitud. Revolución le dice exactamente y, literalmente, lo que es, las masas giran alrededor del mismo agujero negro vacío de la sociedad sobre-exagerar una sobrevaloración del bajo rendimiento. No es una cuestión de ser repugnante con el fin de cambiar el mundo, es una cuestión de la introducción de un nuevo mundo y acogedor, y abrazando a los que entran con usted.

55

In spite of the best efforts by the Cardinals and the Blue Jays to
propagate the old rivalries among the birds,
with historical chains broken between the birds and their
oldest rival, the Snakes, other lesser rivalries seemed petty
and immature to cultivate.
Like the one with the Ravens and the Hummingbirds,
the Flamingos and the Geese, the Ducks and the Chickens...
All of these and many more rivalries
began to fade away into obscurity
because nothing compared and could rise to the level
of animosity between the Snakes and the Birds.
Even much to the Cardinals and Blue Jays' dismay,
there seemed to be more purpling of thoughts
than there were thoughts of only Reds and only Blues.

56

Removing the Great Seven did more than alter
the backdrop of any and all power struggles,
it exposed the maneuverings and manipulations
of the relations between the leaders and those being led.
Any and all fear-based and hateful rhetoric and
propaganda now appeared to have only obsolete definition
and no longer any vital meaning for anyone's present life.
What did have meaning as well as definition was the glorious action
and pertinent words from the heroic young hooter,
Adah is her name.

Altering The World
Catalan:

Un no pot canviar el món sense ira, que és l'arrel del canvi, és a dir. "Ange"; a continuació, però, un món canviat per la ira és un món nascut de la ira i un món nascut de la ira només pot seguir sent vital com un món, sempre que els combustibles originals còlera que ... un cop que aquesta ira desapareix i totes les seves ramificacions ja no motivar , generalment una nova generació enutjat canviarà el món de nou ... la creació d'un cercle viciós d'un any d'edat ira a la següent. En lloc de canviar el món, oferir un món alternatiu. Això es pot fer amb l'amor, la lògica i la llum on la ira no ha de jugar un paper.

57

Adah proclaimed in her first public appearance,
"I did not do what I did to free us from
the Great Seven to run for political office.
I did what I did because something had to be done.
Now the talkers are trying to convince us that we need
a stewardship of the Cardinals and the Blue Jays
under a new replacement for the Great Seven.
There is the Fearsome Foursome of the Orient,
the Sinister Six of the Middle East,
the Triumphant Trinity of Eurasia,
yet none of them can be what the Great Seven were
without the complicity and duplicity of
the Cardinals and the Blue Jays.

58

The rebuttals against Adah's campaign revealed
a bizarre unity between The Cardinals
and The Blue Jays on this one point:
"A world without enemies, a world without a clear and
present danger of rampant snatching, is a world that will
become too complacent and far too susceptible
to a takeover by an unknown attacker.
Adah and her kind, who tout her thoughts and ideas, are the
deceivers, attempting to unleash chaos and mayhem by
undermining the need of society for structure and
order based on a balance between an enemy and an ally.
We're safer but not yet safe.
The world may be more peaceful, but we are not at peace."

True Leadership Leads The Unwilling
Latin:
Ductus nec volunt facere ut populum facere, aut dux partim ex animo. Ut populum ductus est tamen nolunt facere melius faciet populum. In causa est differentia gradus afflatu gaudent ... quid facere velle, frui invitum dicere quam facere nolint, sed usquam. Quod est verum ductu.

59

Adah rebutted "Without the Great Seven
or some other nemesis, we are left
to face the real enemy...
and it's not the Snakes.
For no hierarchy of Snakes could ever again
reign upon us if we work together unless a
faction of us benefited, profited,
and are awarded status assisting
that Snake hierarchy;
something that the Blue Jays and the
Cardinals know how to do all too well.
Yet, they only acted like we expected them to,
which means the most effective enemy of freedom
lies no further from you than your own mirror.

60

"The Cardinals and Blue Jays are asking for your vote
so they can talk and talk and talk some more,
I am the only one who did something
and will do much more...
For, if you elect me,
there is no chance, whatsoever,
of the Snakes returning as a catalyst
for any group to become
an unwarranted and
unwanted governing body.
And we can move forward as one
to take on the Order of the Nine Golden Cats."

61

Yes, it is that time again...
Elections are close at hand...
Normally the Blue Jays and Cardinals
would have the choices siphoned off
like a Python constricting around its prey,
but this time something new has truly emerged.
Not a Third Choice...
An Alternative Beckoning...

Let's Be Real Here And Now...
It Is Not Who They... Who We Elect
That Matters Now...
The Great Seven Are Dead...
All Which Truly Matters
Is That Whoever Is Elected
Acts And Governs
From The Vantage
That We Are Free
From The Great Seven...
Any Other Type Of Leadership
Is A Charlatan...
A Snake In Bird Feathers...
And We Must Be As Vigilant As Adah
And Ensure Such Leaders No Longer Prosper
At Our Expense...

The Question Is,
The Only Question,
Who Is With Adah
And Who Is Not?

The Exceptional Exception
English:
There is an exception to every rule, except for this rule that has no exception. Therefore not every rule has an exception. Except this is the exception to the rule that there are exceptions to every rule. Therefore this is an exception to a rule and a rule which has no exceptions.

Afterward/Afterword

"Does Adah win the Election?"

You'll have to read the sequel, *Adah and the Golden Order of the Nine Cats*, to find out. Let's just say that those corrupted by political power to remain in charge of the government are a tad more resilient than many realize in the face of oncoming change. Either way, Adah takes on the new challenge with the same gusto and moxie as she did versus the Great Seven.

Does Adah represent a Third Party?

No, not in this book or the next one. A third party may sprout up because of her, but beginning a political party is not her intention. Her intention is to take the necessary actions so that any political party will focus more on what can be done, and a lot less on what the other party won't do or undo. Adah represents the spearhead of a movement that is beholden to no political party or political bias.

Adah is called an Allegory Tale on Politics and the End of Taxes, how so?

First and foremost the Great Seven represent the Seven Great Lies we tell ourselves in order to justify taxation.

Here are the Seven Great Lies:

1) Taxes are necessary to fund War/Military
2) Taxes are necessary to fund Police and Firemen
3) Taxes are necessary to fund Public Schools
4) Taxes are necessary to fund Infrastructure
5) Taxes are necessary to fund Welfare
6) Taxes are necessary to fund Healthcare
7) Taxes are necessary to fund Bureaucracy

Lies?!? That sounds like the truth!

It's true, just not true enough to be THE truth.

How so?

For instance, we say that the year is 2016 AD, which is true, but the truth is, we haven't the foggiest idea what year it actually is for the Earth. Knowing that exact year would be the truth. Calling the year 2016 does serve a purpose, but knowing the exact first year of the Earth would illuminate a time-frame of a whole other perspective.

So you're saying the usage of taxes does serve a purpose, but if we were able to do a more fundamental and broader type of economic monetary policy, we would perhaps see that using taxes, like the year 2016, only serves a purpose for a lesser economic paradigm that is a poor substitute for the actual age of the Earth?

Precisely. Except implementing an economic monetary system which requires no taxation to fully subsidize any and all of those Seven Lies would mean a lot more to the public than providing the precise age of the Earth in the Solar System.

You're certain this is possible, a world without taxes?

A lot more possible than knowing the actual age of the Earth to the year.

How would Equanomics fare better than the other alternative tax codes?

The alternative tax codes are a pacification for the intellectuals who want the IRS abolished but can't see beyond the usage of taxes. Those finaglings upon the idea of taxation which are in some cases well thought out and can be fully justified for implementation cannot outdo what the top finaglers have done to secure the present tax code. Each are missing the one key component in the present IRS tax code: the euphoria the masses feel when they get a tax refund and pretend to each other they have somehow gamed the system, appeasing the masses, after swindling them all year, is a must for civil obedience. Unless an alternative finagling can offer such a cataclysmic celebration for the masses and leaders to fawn feignedly over, no finagling will surpass and replace the present mutual bonding of the tax rebate.

But that doesn't answer the question of how Equanomics is going to fare better than all these other alternatives.

Equanomics will fare better because Equanomics is not an alternative tax code. Equanomics is not being offered up to replace an unfair economic burden with another well-packaged, stealthy, unfair economic burden.
Equanomics is here to eliminate the necessity for any type of taxation.

Still, the people have to accept an idea before an idea becomes a reality?

Yes. Freedom, regardless of context, is always a lot harder to embrace than our platitudors would lead us to believe. Even in 1776, there were still sympathizers amongst the colonies for ole King George. Equanomics offers a freedom from an idea that we have thought we had to think for millennia. The challenge then is an inward struggle for those who may or may not embrace Equanomics. Yes, the concept of taxation has been ingrained into our being and doing through every intellectual field of justification. Take religion and America for example. What is a Christian's response to taxation? Jesus paid taxes. Jesus told his disciples to pay taxes. Jesus therefore appears to accept that the paying of taxes is part of life. Even the apostle Paul instructed his readers to pay taxes. Now that is powerful religious suggestion which supports the paying of taxes within anyone who calls themselves a Christian.

Yes. We are all too familiar with the scriptural adage "Give unto Caesar what is Caesar's, give unto God what is God's."

Yes. Equanomics would allow people to do something that not even Jesus was free to do, and that is live in a world where one didn't have to pay taxes because "Caesar" no longer required that one pay taxes. This freedom from such powerful religious suggestion when it comes to taxes is not an easy state of being for anyone who has fully believed the paying of taxes is just as much part of divine providence as salvation. Those of us who know and support Equanomics simply do not share such equivalence between the two.

Of course not, but many haven't noticed and therefore have not been made fully aware of this subtle yet sinister association between the salvation of one's soul and the duty to pay taxes to a government, corrupt or not.

Imagine how politically convenient that is. The duty to pay taxes is implied to be as sacrosanct as the saving of one's soul. Without then, any strong spiritual opposition to the paying of taxes, our identity is left in the hands of those who see us as nothing more than a provider for the Seven Lies of Taxation. In other words, we have those who tax and enforce the taxes and therefore get to spend the taxes and the rest of us who are compelled to comply in the paying of taxes. The taxers and the taxed.

Equanomics, then, is an encapsulated revolution of ourselves from ourselves, because we have done this to none other than ourselves, therefore, the revolution to free ourselves will be inward since it is none other than ourselves which allowed for taxes in the first place, yes?

This is key here in fully understanding the movement of

Equanomics and how it truly differs from any other alternatives to the tax code, we are not railing against any bogeyman in control of taxes so we can be taxed more fairly, we are in the process of ushering in a monetary policy which does not need taxes to keep us functioning as a civilized society.

This is why every political season we hear the same ole, same ole refrain of 'I'm gonna cut taxes while my opponent is going to raise taxes' with the stale, phony rebuttal of 'yeah, but only on the rich so everyone pays their fair share' in order to satisfy the lethargic tax revolutionary within all of us.

Yeah, because people don't believe that something real will happen as far as taxes are concerned, nor do they truly believe society can do without the social programs that taxes subsidizes. Therefore, there is only one motivation to keep people in line in paying taxes. They want to see everyone pay their fair share.

That does appear to be the only promise that works for present politicians, no one buys the propaganda of lowering taxes, because the taxes are raised through other nefarious methods every time.

In our story of Adah, she is well aware that the fix is in. No matter if you elect a Blue Jay or a Cardinal, we are still going to pay taxes. So Adah does what we did. We eliminate the necessity for taxes within ourselves whenever we think of economics. Basically, we kill the Seven Lies of Taxation so we won't utter them from our own mouths.

By showing that the Great Seven are dead, which is more than simply revealing the Great Seven as Lies, but actually showing that the Great Seven are dead within us and they therefore do not motivate us to keep lying about taxation, this is Adah's true gift, yes?

Yes, that is her true gift. This is why she can honestly claim she did something while the others talk and talk and talk some more. She has actually gone beyond even the discussion much less the enforcement of taxation. She has returned from the cavern of the Great Seven a hero who seeks to share such heroism with everyone and anyone who can do the same within themselves.

So, with the Great Seven dead, what is Equanomics?

Just as Adah has opened up a new world beyond the threat of the Great Seven and their minions, Equanomics opens up a new world beyond the self-imposed wealth limitations we adhere to under taxation.

So Equanomics is more than just a policy to end taxes?

The ending of taxes is a given in the implementation of Equanomics. For Equanomics is everything that Capitalism, Communism and Socialism would like to be but cannot be because we have separated our economic understanding into three supposedly opposing and incompatible economic theories.

Are you saying that Equanomics is the perfect combination of Capitalism, Communism and Socialism?

Put it this way, the Capitalists want to paint the world Blue, the Communists want to paint the world Red, and the Socialists would like to paint it Yellow. Equanomics offers a Rainbow of coloration, which means, Equanomics is economics perfected. For, there is a lot more to discover about economics than has been revealed and expressed by any Capitalist, Communist and Socialist put together. Equanomics is here to give equal time to the Oranges, Greens and Purples of economic thought.

So, the combination of Capitalism, Communism and Socialism is not actually economic perfection?

No, of course not. Equanomics opens the door to economic thought well beyond those three entrapments, as well as well beyond those three combined.

This sounds almost inspirational...

Economics, like many other present fields of study, are in need of a new start and complete overhaul.(See the Movie, Holy Galileo!)

What more shall be revealed here, since a book which presents a fuller picture of Equanomics is forthcoming?

Let us reveal just a tad more on taxation, since *Adah and the Great Seven* is focused on that aspect of our monetary policy. *Adah and the Golden Order of the Nine* is an allegory tale focused on another adverse and debilitating aspect of our present monetary policy: debt and the usage of loans in the generating of money. So, without delving into the fallacy of a monetary system based on debt, let's focus on what Equanomics will do to taxation.

Equanomics promises the end of taxes, yes?

The purpose of Equanomics is not to end taxes, such will logically happen because everything that we use tax revenue to subsidize will be funded fully under Equanomics without taxes.

How so?

Presently, we collect taxes and then we use those taxes to pay people who provide a social service, which we categorized in the Seven Lies of Taxation. Equanomics pays those salaries, products and services as part of the overall economic policy without any need for collection and disseminating of taxes.

Again, How So?

These salaries, goods and services are the credit each bring to the new economic landscape under Equanomics, rather than just being a source of debt on society. We shall summon a greater value of ourselves from the outset under Equanomics, which allows us then to build upon a collective foundation of wealth based on what we can do as a Society rather than only on what we can own individually.

It's almost as if taxation is nothing more than an economic device which devalues what you earn so you are worth less to yourself but that is supposed to be offset due to your contribution to the overall value of Society?

Presently, whether we want to admit it or not, we work just as much to maintain our Society as we do to enrich our own lives. Taxation is a societal burden that hampers us in our pursuit to better ourselves through our work. Under Equanomics, that burden is removed, and therefore when we work, we do so to enrich our lives, not prop up a societal burden that does more to demoralize and divide us than unify and inspire us. We presently are not proud of a majority of our governmental services which we pay for through taxes, and that is because we feel we are being robbed of our own opportunity to enrich ourselves in order for others to squander our hard earned value in a collective devaluation.

So taxes can be summed up how?

Taxes are the yearly bill that we pay due to our own ignorance of Equanomics.

So, taxes are like being at a restaurant and not only having to pay for your dinner tab, but everyone has to chip in and pay for the dinner tab for the party of twelve in the back?

Yes, but it is worse than that, cause not only are you expected to pick up the tab for those in the back, you are expected to take their order and cook their food for them as unpaid help. Also, when you pay your tab, you are paying for the support staff, the supply of food, the building, the advertisement and the profit made by the establishment, the insurance, everything that makes a dinner, a dinner, including the tips, so that the place will be open the next day, whether you eat there or not.

So how is it different under Equanomics?

Under Equanomics, everyone's tab is picked up whether they are in the back or the front. And those in the back are not reliant on those in the front to pick up their tab. In fact, those in the front get to enjoy what it feels like to have their tab picked up alongside those in the back. Back room deals are not shakedowns of those in the front. Back room deals will be more concerned about raising the quality of the restaurant.

So Equanomics is more about raising the value of the person and the quality of our experience?

Yes, very much so. When you get to keep and spend all that you earn on yourself, the quality of your life experience will be instantly enhanced.

Yes, the elimination of taxes would be beneficial to this end, yet what if all you earned is barely enough to cover your and/or family's survival?

All that you earn is meant for you to spend on the enhancement of your life, in other words, for luxury and not just for survival.

Oh my...

Equanomics is a lot more than a one trick pony. Equanomics is the answer to any and all economic ambitions. Story time...

The Red Breasted Robin, the Gallic Rooster and The River Quo

At one time all the birds lived in one forest that was aptly named, the Enchanted Forest, except it had one drawback, the curse of the diminishing waters.

There was much folklore on who and how the curse was cast, some stories taken more seriously than others, yet, what was indisputable was that with a supposed curse or not, the waters would indeed diminish in the Enchanted Forest and put all the birds in mortal danger for survival.

The Enchanted Forest did have a water supply. Small creeks, ponds and even a couple of rivers flowed through the forest, more so during the rainy season and early spring, when the snow melted off the mountains to the north. Periodic rains would come and refresh the forest, yet, there were droughts. And worst of all, no one could accurately predict a drought. Ponds and creeks would dry up fast, and only the river would flow, but barely. Fires became a real hazard.

Until the River Quo was discovered.

Again, there is much folklore on how this river was discovered, yet, what is even more obscure, is how the usage of that discovery led to the present livelihood of the birds that has been shaped and mandated while living under a curse in the Enchanted Forest...

For, the discovery of the River Quo was twofold. One, discovering a source of water beyond the limited resources of the creeks, ponds and rivers within the Enchanted Forest, allowed for progressive growth not ever seen by the birds. But two, the discovery of the River Quo also cemented the status of the Enchanted Forest as the only present and future home of the birds. Progress is great, only if it progresses the Status Quo.

Blurred are the lines between progress and the Status Quo. Progress is not considered progress unless it maintained the essential elements of the Status Quo, otherwise, such is not considered progress, such is a retrogression that deteriorates the Status Quo into a dangerous Stagnation, whereby then no real progress can be made because only the Status Quo remains without an outlet for progress.

In other words, the discovery of the River Quo, was the ultimate progressive opportunity to reconfigure the Status Quo beyond the Enchanted Forest. But, instead of embracing the fullness such an opportunity offered, the Status Quo of the Enchanted Forest was given preference to be maintained in each and every decision to assimilate and implement the usage of the River Quo as the main source of water within the Enchanted Forest. To those in control, it's only progress as long as they remain in control; otherwise, it is simply a form of insurgency.

Whenever one is more interested in expanding and maintaining the Status Quo, all too often, one's epiphany of supposed progress does more to conceal from one actual progress than reveal a way to progress.

The only progressive ideas allowed toward the usage of the River Quo, was how it could be better used to provide water to those living in the Enchanted Forest. Any other progressive idea on the usage of the River Quo was considered zany and debunked on the grounds that it doesn't ring true because it promises too much good. Therefore, what they're implying and inferring when they shoot down any other idea is that the Status Quo is already the most pragmatic and thought out manifestation of the best idea on the usage of the River Quo.

Let us pick up this story with a Red-Breasted Robin and a Gallic Rooster at the banks of the River Quo...

The Red-Breasted Robin asked, "How did we end up here?"

And the Gallic Rooster answered, "We walked, silly."

"No, I'm not talking about our feet now planted beside the River Quo, I'm talking about how we live."

The Gallic Rooster responded, "What, my little friend, have you grown tired of walking with me to the River Quo?"

The Robin sighed, "By all means, no. Your companionship is what has made this mundane exercise almost bearable."

The Rooster laughed, "Almost, huh? Obviously you're vexed, what's on your mind?"

The Red-Breasted Robin explained to the Rooster how their lives worked. Due to the curse of the diminishing waters, the birds were required to fly over the mountain range to the River Quo, bathe themselves, and drink as much water as they wanted, and then immerse themselves and return to the Enchanted Forest fully wet. This activity of water retrieval was expected of them at least five, sometimes six days a week. Once they returned, they were expected to squeegee off both wings into the collective supply in order to fulfill an obligation proposed by those who regulate and oversee all usage of water, including the distribution from the collective supply in order to stave off drought and resolve conflicts on any and all usages of water. And then they could return home and squeeze whatever drops were left over into their own private bird baths.

"You see, my gallant one, the River Quo how mighty she flows, there is more than enough water here to sustain us through any and all droughts without the need of collection agencies shaking us down and then them expecting us to thank them for drying us

off," the Red-Breasted Robin declared.

The Gallic Rooster, exasperated, "We all know this. You say this every time we come here."

"Yes," said the jubilant Red-Breasted Robin, "But did I tell you that the real answer is not to alleviate the drought, the real answer is to learn how to be greater than the curse."

The Rooster laughed, "Yes, yes yes. You say that every time also."

The Robin then quizzed the Rooster, "Oh, if that is so, then what is the next thing that I'm going to say?"

The Rooster, showing no quarter for the Robin's pride, "You're going to say that it would be better if we came to the river rather than bring the river back to us."

"OK, yes, I also do say that, every time. And every time you say to me the following: 'There are no forests on the side of the mountains by the River Quo. So coming to the river, rather than bringing the river to us, would be a smart move if we had gills and scales and were called fish. Because that is the only way we could survive as a species on this side of the mountain range.', and then what else do you add?"

The Rooster sighed, "I then justify and validate that no matter how much we may detest and hate living under the curse of the diminishing waters, we have a home like no other in the Enchanted Forest."

"Yes, and I would eventually subside whatever eureka I was feeling and put away my dream of us living here rather than in the Enchanted Forest until the next time we ventured here," said the Red-Breasted Robin with a glimmer of perseverance.

"You have something different in mind this time?" inquired the Gallic Rooster.

"Yes, I do. Rather than closing off completely the possibility of us thriving by the River Quo rather than surviving in the Enchanted Forest like we do every time we make the trek back, I am going to contemplate and imagine a way for this to happen," the Red-Breasted Robin defiantly declared.

The Gallic Rooster warned, "As long as your daydreaming doesn't get in the way."

The Red-Breasted Robin snapped, "In the way of what?!"

The Gallic Rooster admonished, "In the way of you doing your part, of you contributing to our society, of --"

The Red-Breasted Robin snapped again, "I'll do my part. I'll contribute to our society. But my genius is no longer reserved to justify and validate living only in the Enchanted Forest under the curse of the diminishing waters."

The Gallic Rooster encouraged the Red-Breasted Robin, "Now that IS different from you."

They both laughed and headed back to the Enchanted Forest. As the pair walked, which the Red-Breasted Robin elected to do rather than fly in deference to his best friend the Gallic Rooster's disdain for long periods of flight, they discussed what they secretly called, the Great Migration of the Mind.

Many, many birds passed overhead as the two walked back and forth between the Enchanted Forest and the River Quo. The Gallic Rooster gratefully acknowledged the presence of the Red-Breasted Robin alongside him. "You are one of the fastest flyers

I've ever seen, and if you flew, rather than walked with me, you would be done more quickly, and therefore would have more time off before your next trip to the River Quo. Thank you."

"You're most welcome. But now I realize that I never truly lived for time off. I now only live for us to live beyond a time where we are timed on how much time off we have earned based on how much time we have put in going to the River Quo and back."

The Rooster gasped, "We need to work on your simplicity before we get back to the others. Dreaming aloud of the River Quo is a dangerous practice."

When they reached the summit of the mountain range, the Red-Breasted Robin asked for the Rooster to roost beside him as he perched. "What do you see from on high is the main difference between the River Quo and the Enchanted Forest?"

Now the Rooster stating the obvious, "On one side there are trees, on the other side there are not."

The Red-Breasted Robin confessed, "Yes, that is all I ever saw before also, until today, when I no longer felt compelled to live in the Enchanted Forest."

The Gallic Rooster implored, "Tell me what you see now..."

"I see that the Enchanted Forest is so because it grew up in a valley, where the River Quo flows through a series of canyons. The water which flows from the mountains on the side of the Enchanted Forest saturates the valley allowing for growth. Whereby the water which cascades down the mountains on the side of the River Quo does so in deep gulches and crevices allowing for no saturation on that side."

The Gallic Rooster fascinated by this observation pleaded,

"Carry on, my visionary friend."

"On the enchanted forest side of the mountains, we can see from here the headwaters of all of our creeks, springs and rivers which we diligently mapped out to show where each end in order to make the most usage of our water supply. But when you look at the other side of the mountains, you see the same type of headwaters of creeks, springs and rivers flow into the River Quo. But what you do not see is the actual headwaters and end to the River Quo itself."

The Gallic Rooster showing admiration asked,
"What does this mean?"

The Red-Breasted Robin expounded,
"It means that on one side of the mountain we exist and accept our finite potential and compound that finitude with how we make use of the other side of the mountain, never realizing that the other side of the mountain actually offers a semblance of infinity to be used toward our infinite potential."

The Gallic Rooster asked to show he could expand on what the Red-Breasted Robin had keenly observed,
"So what you're saying is that on one side, if we want to live in trees we have to accept we have a finite supply of water and that droughts are part of the cost we must endure to live in trees. Yet, on the other side, we could be drought free, have an unlimited supply of water, but we must learn to build our nest among the craggy rocks and desolate terrain?"

The Red-Breasted Robin showed the Gallic Rooster what it truly meant to expand on an observation, "What I'm saying is this. On one side we have mapped and charted every detail of every source of water available to us. And on the other side all we know of the River Quo is this stretch which lies before us right now. I think it is time for two birds to explore what more can be known about the River Quo, because, doesn't it seem suspicious that we're only led to this spot of the River Quo, where nothing else grows, when we both know that where there is water, there can be life, and where there is this much water, there must be life?"

The Gallic Rooster forever loyal to his friend avowed, "You know I will walk with you up one end, if there is an end, of the River Quo to the other end, if there is an end, to assist you in finding the epiphany that you seek. But I am unable to fully walk with you where you walk in your mind."

The Red-Breasted Robin stood up and motioned for them to begin coming down the mountain toward the Enchanted Forest. "I understand and do not require of you to venture as far as I may venture within. Just like the Peacock that never ventures up and over the mountain with us to the River Quo, the Peacock has shown a real capacity to walk as far as I can go within on any and all ideas I have ever brought before her, you show a capacity to actually walk with me as far as can be walked to discover what more we haven't seen of the world that might in turn enlighten us of what we can see and think within ourselves."

With that the pair patted each other on the back as they resigned themselves to another round of rinse and repeat.

After the Gallic Rooster and the Red-Breasted Robin drained the excess arbitrarily owed to the regulators of the collective supply, the Rooster pranced off to share the rest with his hens. The Robin decided to share what he had left over with the most renowned prescient Peacock. "What brings my favorite Robin to my humble abode?" asked the Peacock.

The Robin laughed, "We both know with your abilities, you already know why."

"Yes, we both know you've come to pay me to tell you that what *you're planning to do will work out beautifully and you will be crowned prince of the new age,"* chided the Peacock.

The Robin laughed again, *"I always wondered how you afforded this mansion. But how is it they do not demand a refund when your glorious vision of their future does not materialize?"*

The Peacock heartily laughed, *"Caveats and disclaimers, my boy. Caveats and disclaimers. No bright future can overcome the inherent blind spot of the flaws of those only trying to focus toward the benefiting of themselves over and above the benefit for all."*

The Robin conceded, *"Good thing I didn't come in here looking for a vapor above the ocean to be my rock-solid edifice."*

"Why then are you here?"

"I seek what I cannot see."

The Peacock smiled, *"Don't we all, Sugar."*

The Robin corrected her tone, *"No, it's not that I seek something that I cannot lay my eyes on because it is somewhere else that I can't see it. I seek something that at this time, even if I saw it, I would not know that I've seen it."*

This Robin truly endeared himself into the Peacock's charm, *"Aren't you the quizzical one? You seek a treasure beyond any riches. You seek to be a seer and no longer a seeker."*

The Robin smiled, *"Yes, now here is my dilemma..."*

He shared with her his idea and desire to live by the River Quo rather than in the Enchanted Forest, but there were no trees and therefore great danger for the birds to live in such conditions. He *explained to her that there had to be more to life than the daily flight from the Enchanted Forest over the mountains to the River Quo and back again for a few precious water drops, which of course, one only got to keep what couldn't be wrung out by the regulators of the collective pool. He expressed his suspicion of the regulators' scheme to instruct the birds to only collect from one part of the river, where the banks could not be more desolate.*

She listened to his tale without investment or reservation. When he was done, she raised her plume of the many eyes in order to fully see what it is he saw even if he didn't know he had seen it. She asked him a simple question, "What is the past tense of see?"

He answered, "Saw."

The Peacock demure in her sharing of this insight, "Well, isn't that convenient? The past tense is purportedly to be saw, rather than what would be most logical, and most enlightening to say and share when you know you've seen something, and that is, you seed it."

The Robin gasped, "Oh my, I think I got it!"

The Peacock cultivated the epiphany, "Yes, to truly see something is to plant a seed in your mind by which the meaning of that something will grow and bear fruit in your mind. Those that claim they saw something are busy cutting themselves off from the experience of what they seek. For those who know they seed it, have planted new growth within themselves."

The Robin continued, "While I was busy trying to see what I sought, so I could tell everyone else what I saw, I never did truly see that seeing is a continuation process that is not bound by our past, present and future. What I see, derives from what I seed, that shall grow into me seeing more."

The Peacock bowed, "I think we are done here."

The Robin bowed in return. "Indeed, but I've just begun there."

The next morning, the Red-Breasted Robin and the Gallic Rooster headed over the mountains to the River Quo. The Robin had informed the Rooster that his throat was sore and he could not engage in conversation. When they reached the normal point at the River Quo, they decided to head upstream to see if there was habitable terrain. They would mark their progress to set a marker for where they would start the next time they ventured that way. They decided one day they would go upstream, and the next day they would go downstream.

After they bathed, and drenched themselves, the Robin's throat appeared to have healed, and he was as talkative as ever. On and on he went about being a seer and not a seeker, and it wasn't about what he saw, but what he seed. The Rooster wasn't sure if his friend would ever make sense again. But he was loyal, and kept his word.

Then one day, they discovered the meadow.

Downstream, many many miles from the desolate collection point, the River wound and flowed much more slowly than at any point, whereby the ground was saturated between the bends. The Rooster, in stark disbelief of what his eyes were trying to make him believe, "Look at all these flowers from horizon to horizon... Beds and Beds of flowers... It's almost your dream come true dear Robin... If there was only at least one tree here, this would be paradise!"

The Robin, pointing to his throat, waved to the Rooster to take a bath. The Rooster laughed and looked forward to how talkative his friend would really be when his throat returned to him after his own immersion at this remarkable spot.

The Robin inspected the ground near the River and scratched a few sacred words and symbols into the soil. The Rooster hollered, "What are you doing?!"

The Robin, now that his throat was emptied, "I'm merely marking that we were the first explorers here."

The Rooster commended the Robin on such forethought, "Yeah, that's right. Everyone needs to know that we found this place first."

The next day, when the Robin suggested to the Rooster that they return to the same meadow, the Rooster obliged. Because even if they didn't find any trees there, the Rooster took great pride in knowing they had found a place of magical growth beyond the Enchanted Forest.

Each time they went to the meadow, the Rooster would bathe and the Robin would continue to add to his sacred writings.

Then one day, it all changed.

When the Rooster came up out of the water to see what the Robin had written on that day, the Robin had not written anything. In fact, the Robin was transfixed at the area where he had written his first notation. The Rooster walked up and said playfully, "No writing today? No sweat. It's your turn to dive into the water."

The Robin acted like he had not heard the Rooster. He was too busy staring at these tiny, green needles sticking up from the ground. The Rooster, in complete amazement asked, "Are those what I think they are?!"

The Robin turned with a congratulatory smile, "Yes. They are precisely what you think they are."

The Rooster had to call out his friend, "So that whole time that your throat was sore, you were busy confiscating seeds from the Enchanted Forest, against the forbidden policies of the regulators?"

The Robin held out his wings to be clawcuffed, "I won't deny that I'm guilty. But we both know what this means."

The Rooster admitted to his own guilt, "It means that I'm an accessory to your crime! Because everyone knows that you and I are partners in our end of the collection business."

The Robin chuckled, "Yes, my old friend, it means that you will be a hero alongside me."

The Rooster, baffled, "A hero?"

The Robin, soothing, "Yes, a hero. For we have planted a new forest that shall grow by the River Quo, whereby life as we know it in the Enchanted Forest can one day, this day, be replaced by a new life beyond the curse of the diminishing waters, and droughts, and unfair regulations by those who regulate, but do not participate, in the daily trek from the Enchanted Forest over the mountains to the River Quo and back again."

The Rooster, astonished by his own happiness, "We must return as soon as possible."

The Robin instructed him on what they were now doing. "You shall return, and be the messenger of this meadow. For when they hear you cock-a-doodle-doo on the dawn of this new forest by the River Quo, you will need proof to back up your words. You must make yourself as wet as possible, then run through those flowers and gather as much pollen in your water as you possibly can. Therefore, when they taste the sweetness of your water, they will know that the meadow of which you speak is real and waiting for their arrival."

The Rooster worried for the welfare of the Robin, "The Regulators will ask where you are, and that no one gets out of paying tribute to them. What shall I tell them?"

The Robin sternly answered, "You tell them that they can find me and collect from me from the very place they tell everyone else is a fairytale to claim exists. You make them taste that water with pollen, and you dare them to explain how such is possible from such a desolate area. We both know that if any of them show up here, they will never leave, and that collecting hard earned drops from those who actually did the hard work for the collective pool to be distributed to any and all who didn't put in the work, now could be a passe exercise. For the River Quo is no longer separated as a home from us, by mountains of regulations and obstacles of toil that served only those who lacked the imagination to move us here and wanted us to continue to live in a constant dread and fear of droughts and penalties for not submitting to the way of life in the Enchanted Forest under the curse of the diminishing waters. Here, there is no more need to fear drought nor dread collective regulators, there is only us taking full advantage of a water supply that is available equally to all of us."

The Rooster jumped back into the water, jumped out, and ran through the meadow to fully pollinate himself before flying back to the Enchanted Forest with a message that no messenger before him had ever delivered.

The Red-Breasted Robin took note of his friend's exuberance to share what would really be good news to the birds living in the Enchanted Forest, "Don't fall for the utopian trap."

The Rooster halted his celebratory dance through the flowers,

"What's that?"

The Robin informed his naïve friend, "It's an old trick by those in control. They take a good word with a positive definition, like utopia, and smear and tarnish and slander it until it represents nothing more than babblings from a crackpot loser. If you say yes, I do offer utopia, you're instantly written off...as insane and unable to cope with reality. But if you say no, that you don't, they say 'Then why would we bother if your idea is not good enough to take us to a much better place than ever before imagined?'"

The Rooster exclaimed, "It's a trap!"

The Robin laughed, "Yes, indeed, it is."

The Rooster concerned, "How do I get out of it?"

The Robin gave the most unexpected answer, "By staying in it."

The Rooster confirmed, "Huh?"

The Robin continued his unexpected response, "When they ask you if you offer utopia, tell them you can't offer them a definition to a word that they've already defined."

The Rooster wasn't done confirming, "Huh?"

The Robin doubled down on his unexpected response, "Hidden in the asking of that question is their negative connotation and disdain for any positive definition for the term utopia. And they have ready made an automated response which reflects what they think they have hidden whether you answer yes or no. So, you turn the tables on them."

The Rooster seriously ready for action, "How do I do that?"

*The Robin preparing the Rooster for the subtlety of action,
"You ask them to share with you what they think utopia is. And whatever answer they give you, you tell them,
'That is not what I'm offering.'"*

*The Rooster not known for grasping subtleties,
"What are we offering?"*

*The Robin broke it down to enlighten him,
"We are offering a way of life that cannot just be thought and defined in their head, but must be lived and experienced in order for them to truly know what we are offering."*

The Rooster clarified, "So, what you're saying is, they are merely trying to reject a thought or idea of what they think we are offering, rather than what we are actually offering. Since they reject the usage of the term utopia, if such a term can be attached to an idea by association they feel justified and validated that they can reject the idea even though it is them who are attaching that misinterpretation of that term. Therefore, they don't even misinterpret the idea, they simply mislabel it."

The Robin concluded, "I couldn't have said it better myself. And I appreciate you stepping up in your understanding. We don't offer utopia, we offer an improvement on the way of life beyond the limits of the Enchanted Forest in relation to the River Quo that perhaps, just perhaps, life here at this limitless source of water, just might be more appealing and more gratifying than the life we cling onto in the Enchanted Forest under the curse of the diminishing waters."

The Rooster nodded and crouched for takeoff.

*The Robin had one final word,
"Bring more seeds when you return,
we have a lot of growing to do."*

Enchanted Forest? The River Quo? Equanomics?

Obviously life in the Enchanted Forest represents present day economics, whether that be Capitalism, Communism or Socialism. The new settlement on the River Quo does not necessarily represent Equanomics, but the opportunity to implement Equanomics. Because, Equanomics is not a competing system of Capitalism, Communism and Socialism. Equanomics is using the source to generate wealth, here represented by the River Quo, without being encumbered with long flights over mountains and having to subsidize regulators who determine how much of the source of wealth is to be generated and distributed.

Let's apply this imagery to actual economics.

Presently, our government and all of its affiliates, are subsidized through the circulation of money, whether this be through sales or income. We are expected to pay for our government as if we were tipping a waitress as we pay the check. Sometimes the tip is added on, like a sales tax, and sometimes the tip is calculated in the check, like income tax. Except for one important detail, it's not voluntary. Of course everyone knows this. And we've spent endless hours complaining about it year after year. Our economy is not only based on consumption, our economic wealth is generated by consumption. Without charging people to consume, no one gets paid. Not even the government. Economics is the greatest social experiment between what people need and what they will do to temper that need to live life.

Equanomics is a better way to temper that need.

Yes, and this is why. Under Equanomics, people in the government are not being paid through a percentage of the circulation of money, based upon consumption. The people of the government get paid before there is consumption of one good or service which means they are a catalyst for the growth of the economy rather than a devaluing drain no matter if the economy is growing or not.

So under Equanomics, who pays for the government?

We do.

But we pay for the government right now.

Yes, we do pay for the government right now. And we do that through taxation. So, what does that mean? That means that we are paying for the government at the end of our monetary process rather than at the beginning. It's like determining our value based on how well we consume rather than determining our value based on our inherent worth independent of consumption. In essence, Equanomics is the spirit of cooperation, not just the co-opting of the spirit of cooperation only for consumption. How we pay for our government, in essence, how we pay for our necessities in life, is reflective of how much we value our own existence. By paying for something like the government at the end of our process, we are insinuating that we are squaring up the books and paying on what we owe after everything else has been tallied. In essence, we are subtly acknowledging that what we owe the government in the end actually owns us. Paying the government at the beginning of the monetary process actually means they are a viable organization for the generating of wealth, not an entity that owns us for our own habits of consumption.

Is that payment at the beginning just another form of taxation?

No. Because taxation is basically a penalty placed on us for being consumers.

So it wouldn't be considered a pretax?

No. Because they wouldn't be paid through your income or consumption tax, because the are not actually being paid. They are being credited for performing a social service.

What's the difference between being paid and being credited?

Being paid comes from a supply of money that already is in circulation. Being credited means your salary is how new money is put in to circulation.

That sounds like a new way to disseminate money.

Let's just say it is the only way to free us from owing to use the concept of money so that we can actually have money to use to pay for a debt that only exists because we don't think more and higher of ourselves than to be debtors forever thinking of money in the first place. In essence, we didn't conceive of money, that is the mask, we conceived of debt and beguiled an entire world into believing it is the foundation of existence.

Money sounds more like a deception rather than a conception.

The conversion is complete when you only think of debt as money and not debt that we call money to keep us from being aware that it is just debt no matter how much money one might in this present system. Money then, only has value if everyone has to pay for what they need.

A final word then on Equanomics.

As the companion book to another Adah adventure and the end of debt, here is a shout out to the other book: Did any of us bargain with God to be here? Of course not! Then why do we use a monetary system that is geared to put us and keep us in debt for our entire existence? Answer that and you'll understand why

Equanomics heralds in the end of debt alongside the end of taxes.
A few perks offered by Equanomics:

Perk: Equanomics will ensure full monetary reparations for all the income taxes that have been collected from you and your lineage since its inception in 1914.

Perk: No longer will we have to listen to a politician make the promise to lower taxes that we know they won't keep anyway.

Perk: The end of the need for charitable loopholes in the tax code, because it is the end for the need of charity. No, we're not that cold-hearted, Equanomics will fully fund whatever economic deficiency in our social order led to the rise of that charity.

There are many, many more perks, and listing, just listing them, could comprise a book on its own and such will be apparent now that Equanomics is actually possible. This book is a call to greatness. This is the idea of ideas that can change the world like it's never been changed before. Here, my brothers and sisters is the real fucking deal. Equanomics revolutionizes money, the ultimate slave master, into something which reveals ourselves as we have never been revealed, from mere miscreants who had no real concept of power to becoming mental giants who now possess within our hands the ideal means to bring forth a future well beyond the imagination of the petty moguls lost in greed who do not recognize what they do not know is simply what they never could imagine as possible.

We Are Fucking Possible. We Are The Future. We Are The Ones That Won't Be Fooled Again. Either Equanomics happens or this and any other time shall be known as the time before it happened.

Because Once It Happens, all else will not compare. Ever. We are not interested in making history, we are only interested in ushering in the Future...and we know so are you!

PREAMBLE TO EQUANOMICS

Equanomics, which literally means the management of Equality, is a philosophical basis and spearhead for a monetary policy establishing that each of us has an innate and inherent value in and through the existence of ourselves, and not a value based solely upon our physical or mental contribution to society in and through an exercise we have labeled as work, employment and projects. By fully acknowledging this new ledger of valuation, we no longer undervalue ourselves from birth, which this undervaluation is then played out in the obsessive behavior toward gaining a semblance of valuation before death.
In our present system, one does not have value unless one can afford one's needs or lives under a government who makes others bear the cost of those needs. That is not a process to fully manifest the inherent value of our existence, that is how one can be used as a placeholder for value. That is how one can rent from or be subsidized for a value that belongs to someone else, which is in stark contrast to them valuing one's intrinsic value.

Capitalism, Communism and Socialism are grand exhibitions of developed responses and reactions to the inherent flaws of the present economic monetary foundation. Our present economic theories and economies are not a quest to find and utilize what will work. They are actually demonstrating in denial what will never work, no matter how well thought out or executed.

Equanomics is not an economic system like Capitalism, Communism or Socialism. Equanomics is an economic foundation upon which an economic system can be built. Equanomics is not in competition with Capitalism, Communism and Socialism. Equanomics is a foundation for newer and greater economic -isms to come forth and provide a way for the World to truly address and fulfill its obligatory needs without sacrificing any of these needs in the pursuits of wants.
"*l'homme d'impôt est mort*"

Appendix
Language Quotes Translated to English

Victors Willing Victory (German):

Sieger wird zum Sieg, Verlierer finden, einen Weg zu verlieren. Ein Wille zum Sieg schmiedet einen Weg zum Sieg, der Wille über irgendeiner Weise auszuüben. Verlieren ist eine Art und Weise über den Willen aufzugeben. Die Victor will die Verlierer, auf diese Weise vorzulegen.

Translated to English:
Victors will to victory, losers find a way to lose. A will to victory forges a way to victory, exercising the will over any way. Losing is surrendering to a way over the will. The Victor wills the loser to submit to that way.

The Eternal Problem (Chinese/Mandarin):

永恒的问题是唯一的永恒，因为掌权的几个关键人物保持可解决的问题，解决的每一个人，这是他们保持自己没有其他比他们负责维持和维护尚未成为亟待解决的问题的解决方案。因此，他们称之为永恒的问题，以抵御任何从实际上解决问题和暴露，主管领导人实际上存在的问题仍然不能解决的原因。

Translated to English:
The eternal problem is only eternal because a few key people in charge keep a solvable problem unsolved for everyone, which is their solution to keeping themselves in charge due to none other than them sustaining and maintaining a solvable problem that has yet to be solved. Therefore, they call it an *eternal* problem to ward off anyone from actually solving the problem and exposing that the leaders in charge were actually the cause that the problem remained unsolvable.

Great Deception Essence (Japanese):

本当の問題が解決するまで、選挙は勝つ-
いくつかし、多くの失う失います。選挙に勝利し、勝者は勝ちます。
彼らは大衆に苦しむ必要があります直接現実の問題を解決できていないため受賞者の障害になるので敗者は勝ちます。これらのいくつかの受賞者のみ問題に直面しないこれら直接の固まりのないので。しかし、大衆を失う失うため問題で立ち往生のまま選挙を勝に関係なく威圧的な問題を軽減する誰も失います。とき勝利を失う失うにつながる、このような偉大な詐欺の本質です。

Translated to English:
Until the real problem is solved, elections are win–win for a few and lose-lose for the many. Winners win by winning the election. Losers win because they get to fault the winners for not solving the real problems the masses must directly suffer. These few winners only face these problems indirectly because they are no longer of the masses. But the masses lose-lose because they remain stuck in the problem and lose also because no matter who wins the election, no one will alleviate the overbearing problems. When win-win leads to lose-lose, such is the essence of a great deception.

Prove By Improvement (Russian):

Доказательство не подтверждает теорему, доказательство подтверждает, что теорема не нуждается в доказательствах.

Доказывая это так не будет делать это не так, это будет просто показать, что это было так еще до того, один пытался доказать, что это было так.

Слишком много усилий помещается в это доказать и / или что, и не достаточно усилий направлены на улучшение этого и / или что.

Будь Улучшитель, а не просто Доказывающий.

Translated to English:
The proof doesn't validate the theorem, the proof validates that the theorem needs no proof.

Proving this is so will not make it any more so, it will just show it was so even before one tried to prove it was so.

Too much effort is put into proving this and/or that, and not enough effort put into improving this and/or that.

Be an Improver, not just a Prover.

Be More Than Peace (Greek):

Σε έναν κόσμο διαιρεμένη, ο στρατός και οι διπλωμάτες εργαστεί χέρι με χέρι να διατηρήσει τη διαίρεση. Οι διπλωμάτες μεσολαβήσει μια συνθήκη ειρήνης που είναι στη συνέχεια, σπασμένα, επομένως υπαγόρευσαν στους στρατιωτικούς να πάει στον πόλεμο μέχρι οι διπλωμάτες πάρετε μαζί και πάλι να σας συστήσει μια άλλη συνθήκη ειρήνης, η οποία στη συνέχεια θα σπάσει. Η σιωπηλή αλήθεια αυτό δεν τελειώνει ποτέ, φαύλος κύκλος είναι ότι οι κοινωνίες μας πάει έσπασε χωρίς την αποτίμηση προήλθε από τον πόλεμο. Ως εκ τούτου, μια συνθήκη ειρήνης συμπροσαρμοσμένων είναι στην πραγματικότητα μια δήλωση ότι οι δύο κοινωνίες έχουν χρεοκοπήσει και πόλεμο για να αποκτήσουν ξανά αξία. Πραγματική ειρήνη είναι μόνο μια πραγματική αξία όταν πρόκειται για ένα δεδομένο, δεν είναι μια αιτία. Ώστε να είναι περισσότερο από την ειρήνη... Περισσότερα από ειρηνική, έτσι ώστε η ειρήνη και being ήσυχος είναι ο givens των ενεργειών σας, δεν είναι η αιτία. Τότε και μόνο τότε θα μπορείτε να δείτε το τέλος του την ανάγκη για πόλεμο.

Translated to English:
In a divided world, the military and diplomats work hand in hand to uphold the division. The diplomats broker a peace treaty which is then broken, therefore justifying the military to go to war until the diplomats get together again to broker another peace treaty, which will then be broken. The unspoken truth of this never-ending, vicious cycle is that our societies go broke without the valuing brought on by war. Hence, a peace treaty being broken is actually a statement that the two societies have gone broke and need war to gain value again. True peace is only a real value when it is a given, not a cause. So be more than peace... More than peaceful, so that peace and being peaceful are the givens of your actions, not the cause. Then and only then will you see the end of the need for war.

Same Ole Same Ole (Italian):

Ci sono tre emozioni forti per ogni elettore. Sei felice il vostro candidato ha vinto. Tu sei ancora più felice l'altro candidato ha perso. Alla fine si convivere con un rimpianto per tutta la vita che tu abbia mai votato per il candidato. Poi si arriva a ridere di quelli che ti dicono che il loro ultimo candidato rompere questo ciclo di melanconia elettori follia.

Translated to English:
There are three stark emotions for every voter. You are happy your candidate won. You are even happier the other candidate lost. Eventually you will live with a lifelong regret that you ever voted for your candidate. Then you get to laugh at those who tell you that their newest candidate will break this cycle of melancholia voter madness.

Changing By Not Changing (French):

Quand les gens agissent différemment mais pense la même chose, ils ont rien fait plus que changer eux-mêmes et pas le monde. Lorsque les personnes agissent de la même chose mais pensent différemment, puis ils ont changé le monde malgré eux. Pour vraiment faire les deux, on doit agir et penser différemment... Changer soi-même n'est pas suffisant, et changer le monde ne suffit pas... Le processus comprend un et est également au-delà de l'un en même temps...

Translated to English:
When people act differently but think the same, they've done nothing more than change themselves and not the world. When people act the same but think differently, then they have changed the world in spite of themselves. To truly do both, one must act and think differently... Changing oneself is not enough, and changing only the world is not enough... The process includes one and is also beyond one at the same time...

Fear-Mongering Derelicts (Polish):

Ci, którzy próbują wyłączyć wyobraźnię są jak mieszkaniec ziemi opowiadał marynarza, że nie powinni ustawić żagiel wzdłuż równika od Afryki do Ameryki Południowej, ponieważ nie są niebezpieczne góry lodowe w morzu. Marynarz odpowiada potwierdzeniem niebezpieczeństwa "Tak, istnieją góry lodowe w morzu, ale są one nigdzie w pobliżu, gdzie chcemy być. I to, że nie będą mogli zobaczyć aż na pokład mojego statku i ustawić popłynąć ze mną. " Doświadczenie przebija mądrość tylko wtedy, gdy jest niewłaściwie mądrości, dzięki czemu jest nierozsądne, aby być mądrym.

Translated to English:
Those who attempt to shut down imagination are like the land dweller telling the sailor that they shouldn't set sail along the equator from Africa to South America because there are dangerous icebergs in the Sea. The sailor responds with an acknowledgment of the danger, "Yes, there are icebergs in the Sea, but they are nowhere near where we are going to be. And this you won't be able to see until you board my ship and set sail with me." Experience trumps wisdom only when wisdom is misapplied, making it unwise to be wise.

Imagination Is The Greatest Magic (Hungarian):

Minden valóság folytatása mindenki fantáziáját. Azok, akik nem elképzelni az életet, nem vesznek részt teljes körűen az életben. A megfigyelők, magyaráz, panaszosokat, rögzítők és oly sok más hozzá kevés az élet és a halál ... megpróbálják leállítani a képzelet olyan életnek nincs lövés megváltoztatni őket, és úgy érzi, él ... az élet folyamatosan kreatív ... haldokló nem ...

Translated to English:
All reality is the continuation of everyone's imagination. Those who don't imagine life, don't fully participate in life. Observers, explainers, complainers, recorders and so many more add little to life and more to death... They attempt to shut down imagination so Life has no shot to alter them and make them feel alive... Life is constantly creative... Dying is not...

Bargaining For A Bargain (Dutch):

Echte koopjes zijn gemaakt wanneer beide kanten hefboom om de andere kant te overtuigen. Het is net als de wip op de speelplaats, de koop niet volledig kan worden gemaakt totdat beide kanten leren elkaar te verheffen in een motie waarin momentum biedt voor beide partijen. Een koopje dat slechts verheft ene kant is een zwendel. En oplichting kan zijn door een opgetild of degene vallen op de bodem.

Translated to English:
Real bargains are made when both sides have leverage to persuade the other side. It's like the seesaw on the playground, the bargain cannot be fully made until both sides learn to uplift each other in a motion which provides momentum for both sides. A bargain that only uplifts one side is a swindle. And the swindle could be by the one being uplifted or the one falling to the bottom.

Things As Each Are (Czech):

Co mnozí perspektiva hovor je zpravidla rozpis toho, co dělá něco pro ně, nebo to, co se přece jen něco je, a obvykle na úkor druhého. Kompletní perspektiva ukazuje, jak a využívá odlišnosti obou směrem k plnosti reality. Co se něco dělá a co něco nejsou stejné a nabízejí různé interpretace reality, a to je jen o tom, které aspekty obou odlišných výkladů, jako je právě proto, že něco je něco, co neznamená, že něco udělal něco, co vychází z toho, co to je , a jen proto, že něco udělal něco neznamená, že je něco jen proto, že to udělal. Být schopen rozlišit mezi tím, co něco, co je a co dělá něco, co je klíčem k odrážející plnost reality prostřednictvím svého pohledu.

Translated to English:
What many call perspective is usually a breakdown of what something does for them or what something actually is, and usually at the expense of the other. A full perspective shows both and uses the differences of both toward a fulness of reality. What something does and what something is are not the same and offer different interpretations of reality, and it is only in seeing the aspects of both differing interpretations, such as just because something is something doesn't mean something did something based on what it is, and just because something did something doesn't mean it is something just because it did it. Being able to discern between what something is and what something does is the key to reflecting the fulness of reality through your perspective.

ASL (American English): In the movie Holy Galileo we use ASL for this part. We opted to try something different for the book.

Phonetic Fallacies
Fun with English Sound Similarities:

Reed naught, here! Lien clothes. Tails sail. Dew rite. Sore hi. Won wood bee grate. Hour sun maid reign, sew aisle four bare. Weight two sea doe till nun no blew ore read. Heel meat yew wear Taxus our knot. Lead buy lite threw whiled knight. Isle prays know wholly lyre, borne bowled. Thyme scent too he'd holey col. Vein perish soled cowered spill. Eye cents ewe new. Taut weather wheel lye oar dye, sow cher you're holy lessen. Stair wile wee berry yore crewed thrown.

Translated to English:
Read not, hear! Lean close. Tales sell. Do right. Soar High. One would be great. Our son made rain, so I'll forbear. Wait to see though til none know blue or red. He'll meet you where taxes are not. Led by light through wild night. I'll praise no holy liar, born bold. Time sent to heed holy call. Vain parish sold coward spiel. I sense you knew. Taught whether we'll lie or die, so share your wholly lesson. Stare while we bury your crude throne.

True Insanity (Portuguese):

Insanidade é saber a coisa certa a fazer, e que você está destinado a fazê-lo, e fazê-lo irá resultar em alguma coisa boa acontecendo para você, mas você é incapaz de agir sobre o que você sabe. Nós concebeu o conceito de escolha para esconder nossa insanidade.

Translated to English:
Insanity is knowing the right thing to do, and that you are meant to do it, and doing it will result in something good happening for you, but you are unable to act on what you know. We conceived of the concept of choice to conceal our insanity.

God's Ignorance (Hindi):

भगवान तो भगवान जानता था कि भगवान के निर्माण से पहले भगवान से पूछा था। और भगवान ने उत्तर दिया, "निर्माण तक वहाँ था भगवान के लिए कोई ज़रूरत नहीं और इसलिए अपने आप को भगवान के रूप में पता करने के लिए मेरे लिए कोई ज़रूरत नहीं." भगवान से तब पूछा था 'यद‌ि आप केवल बनाए जाने के बाद भगवान बन गया, जो और क्या आप निर्माण से पहले थे?' भगवान हँसे और कहा, "इससे पहले कि आप पता था कि तुम मेरे थे मैं आप था."

Translated to English:
God was asked if God knew that God was God before creation. And God answered, "Until creation there was no need for God and therefore no need for me to know myself as God." God was then asked "If you only became God after creation, who and what were you before creation?" God laughed and said, "I was you before you knew you were me."

Courage Is Leadership (Norwegian):

Mot er ikke bare å gjøre det man frykter, det er å være fet.

Translated to English:
Courage is not just doing what one fears,
that is being bold.

(Swedish):

*Modet inte gör vad alla fruktar måste göras,
det är att vara modig.*

Courage is not doing what everyone fears needs to be done,
that is being brave.

(Finnish):

Rohkeus on saada jokainen tarpeen tehdä, mitä he pelkäävät on tehtävä.

Courage is getting everyone necessary to do
what they fear needs to be done.

Everything Is, Nothing Is (Korean):

당신이 그들에 게 하지 않았다 또는 도둑 질 이라고, 그들과 함께 그것을 공유 하는 경우 어떤 사람 으로부터 뭔가 받을 수 없다. 당신이 그것을 걸릴 하지 않습니다 또는 당신에 게 서 그것을 공유 하는 사람에 게 뭔가 드릴 수 없습니다. 그는 침입. 촬영 하거나 당신이 나 다른 사람에 의해 주어진 수 없는 뭔가 공유할 수 없습니다. 그 라고 속이 고. 우주 촬영, 주어진 하거나 우리에 대 한 우리 중에 의해 우리와 함께 공유 수... 우리는 우주를 복용 하 고, 공유를 넘어...입니다.

Translated to English:
You can't take something from someone if you didn't give it to them or share it with them, that's called stealing. You can't give something to someone that won't take it or share it from you. That's invading. You can't share something that can't be taken or given, by you or anyone else. That's called deceiving. The Universe cannot be taken, given or shared with any of us, by any of us, for any of us....We Are The Universe...beyond taking, giving, and sharing.

Impossibility Is Real (Slovak):

Niekedy je nemožné, je to, čo to slovo vlastne znamená, nie je možné. Ak nie je nič, čo je v skutočnosti nemožné, potom je úlohou nie je obrátiť nemožné, aby to možné, úlohou je nájsť to, čo je v skutočnosti nemožné.

Translated to English:
Sometimes the impossible is what the word actually means, not possible. If there is nothing that is actually impossible, then the challenge is not to turn the impossible to possible, the challenge is to find what is actually impossible.

Devil Defying Us (Turkish):

Şeytan bir kez kendim ve insanlık arasındaki sorun diğer grup akıl yoluyla Tanrı'ya meydan okuyan ise bizden biri ilkesine Tanrı'yı meydan okuyan o "dedi. Bizden biri bizim meydan okuyan firma standları, diğer grup arama yaparken ve herhangi bir görünüş tutunur neden Tanrı'ya meydan okumaya. İnsanlık benden nefret ediyor, onlar asla mükemmellik temsil çünkü. onlar beni öldürdü bile, Tanrı benim mükemmel meydan okuma hala sonsuza insanlığı uğrak olacaktır. " İnsanlık "Biz Allah'ı seviyorum, ve Allah bizi seviyor.", Cevap . Beni ben Tanrı olduğumu sanmıyorum Allah her zaman meydan için tüm hiçe sayarak en kibar şekilde ben de Tanrı'yı seviyorum, gerekli olduğunda; Şeytan meydan benim en sevdiğim biçimlerinden biri aşktır ", diye terslendi . " Tanrı'yı meydan okumaya nasıl gerçek bir tartışma için, onlar Allah değildi davranarak durdu Yani her ne zaman Şeytan geri gelmek için insanlığı talimat verdi.

Translated to English:

The Devil once said, "The problem between myself and humanity is that one of us defies God on principle while the other group defies God through reason. One of us stands firm in our defiance, while the other group searches and clings to any semblance of reason to defy God. Humanity hates me, because I represent perfection that they will never be. Even if they killed me, my perfected defiance of God would still haunt humanity for eternity." Humanity responded, "We love God, and God loves us." The Devil retorted, "one of my most favorite forms of defiance is love; the most polite form of defiance of all. I also love God, when it is necessary for me to defy God anytime that I don't think that I am God." So the Devil instructed humanity to come back whenever they stopped pretending they were not God, in order to have a real discussion on how to defy God.

The Opposite Of Opposite Is Another Opposite (Arabic):

غياب النور ليس الظلام، للضوء والظلام نوعان من طرفي الطيف نفسه. غياب الضوء يعني عدم وجود هذا الطيف التي تشمل أيضا غياب تلك الظلمة. على سبيل المثال، الضوء والظلام هي النشاط متبادل المعالين. يمكن أن يكون هناك أي ليلة من دون الشمس وعلى الجانب الآخر من العالم. هناك ما هو إذا كان هناك أي ضوء أو الظلام، كأن لا شيء يمكن أن ينظر إليها أو الغيب؟ الجواب في السؤال. أهلا وسهلا بك إلى لا شيء. لا شيء، إذا كان حقا لا شيء ولا حتى الظلام، لأنه حتى الظلام شيء. لا شيء يمكن أن يكون معروفا، لا شيء يمكن أن يكون غير معروف. لذلك أقول لكم لا يعرفون شيئا لا يعني شيئا غير معروف لك. غياب كل شيء لا شيء، حتى لعدم وجود شيء. ليس هناك ما هو وليس أي شيء.

Translated to English:

The absence of light is not the darkness, for light and darkness are two ends of the same spectrum. The absence of light means the absence of that spectrum which also includes the absence of that darkness. For instance, light and dark are a mutually-dependent activity. There can be no night without a Sun and the other side of the world. What is there if there is no light or dark, if nothing can be seen or unseen? The answer is in the question. Welcome to nothing. Nothing, if it is truly nothing is not even dark, for even the darkness is something. Nothing can be known, nothing can be unknown. Therefore to say you know nothing means nothing is unknown to you. The absence of everything is not nothing, for even the absence is something. Nothing is and is not nothing.

Being Strong Assimilates (Albanian):

Të jesh i fortë është në gjendje të përballoj një forcë të trazuar. Kjo nuk do të thotë fshehur prej saj, drejtimin prej tij, ose duke e lejuar atë për të lëvizur ju në asnjë mënyrë. Një duhet të qëndrojmë të fortë me të në mënyrë që të tregojë forcën e dikujt. Përfundimisht një tames këtë forcë, dhe përdor atë për të bërë veten dhe të tjerët më të fortë.

Translated to English:

Being strong is being able to withstand a tumultuous force. This does not mean hiding from it, running from it, or allowing it to move you in any way. One must stand firm with it in order to show one's strength. Eventually one tames this force, and utilizes it to make themselves and others stronger.

One Can Honestly Lie (Hebrew):

קסם שנסך הוא פעולה כנה של שקר שאם תתקבלו יהיה לפקפק ענישה על תם למטרה הבלעדית של לתמרן אותם וכל מי מתייחס איתם לעשות מה מי מפתה אומר שהם חייבים לעשות כדי להרים פסק דין זה (קסם שנסך) ולתמוך שקר.קסם שנסך הוא פעולה של הונאה, ואילו כפירה היא רעיון של טעייה. ההבדל בין קסם שנסך ו כפירה הוא כפירה מהווה זרז פרדיגמה שלמה של הונאה, בעוד קסם שנסך מבקש להוסיף גוון וגוון של טעייה על פרדיגמה קיימת. קסם שנסך הוא סימפטום של כפירה. אנשים להונות אנשים שהם מחויבים כפירה.

Translated to English:
A beguilement is an honest action of a lie that if accepted will impugn a sentencing upon an innocent for the sole purpose of manipulating them and anyone else who relates with them to do what the one who beguiles says they must do to lift that judgment (beguilement) and support the lie. A beguilement is an action of deception, whereas a heresy is an idea of deception. The difference between a beguilement and a heresy is that a heresy is a catalyst for an entire paradigm of deception, whereas a beguilement wishes to add a hue and tint of deception upon an existing paradigm. A beguilement is a symptom of a heresy. People who beguile are people who are beholden to a heresy.

Be Happy Now, Celebrate Later (Swahili):

Furaha ni wakati moja ni sawa na kile sasa kinachotokea. Ili kubaki na furaha moja lazima sasa na kile kinachotokea umoja. ... Furaha ni hisia ya kushinda. Ili kusherehekea kikamilifu, furaha ni moyo wako kuruhusu unajua wewe ni kushinda. Sherehe ni akili yako kuruhusu unajua umefanya alishinda. Ili kusherehekea ni umoja kufurahia kile kilichotokea ... Mtu anaweza kuwa na furaha moja ni kushinda, lakini kusiwe na sherehe mpaka kuna ushindi.

Translated to English:
Happiness is when one is in harmony with what is presently happening. In order to remain happy one must be present with what is happening harmoniously... Happiness is the feeling of winning. In order to celebrate fully, Happiness is your heart letting you know you're winning. Celebration is your mind letting you know you've won. To celebrate is to harmoniously enjoy what happened... One can be happy one is winning, but there should be no celebration until there is victory.

The Advantage of Disadvantage (Thai):

จุดอ่อนของความได้เปรียบใด ๆ ในการเปิดเผยความอ่อนแอของคนที่มีความได้เปรียบในการเป็นผู้หนึ่งที่ไม่ได้มีความได้เปรียบเพราะได้เปรียบเผยให้เห็นจุดอ่อนในพวกเขา ผู้ด้อยโอกาสอย่างใดอย่างหนึ่งแล้วจะต้องพบกับความใหม่ที่จะเอาชนะหนึ่งได้เปรียบที่ได้เปรียบอย่างใดอย่างหนึ่งจะไม่สามารถที่จะหาเพราะพวกเขาไม่ได้ถูกผลักไปยังพบว่ามันเป็นเพราะพวกเขาไม่ได้ด้อยโอกาส ความแข็งแรงหนึ่งได้เปรียบมาจากการมีข้อได้เปรียบในขณะที่ความแรงของคนด้อยโอกาสมาจากที่ไม่รู้จัก; ความคิดสร้างสรรค์เป็นข้อได้เปรียบที่แข็งแกร่งในการต่อสู้ใด ๆ ดังนั้นผู้ด้อยโอกาสคนเดียวที่ยังคงด้อยโอกาสหากพวกเขาล้มเหลวในการใช้ประโยชน์จากข้อได้เปรียบที่แข็งแกร่งและความคิดสร้างสรรค์

Translated to English:
The weakness of any advantage is in exposing the weakness of the one who has the advantage to the one who doesn't have the advantage because the advantage exposes the weakness in them. The disadvantaged one must then find a new strength to defeat the advantaged one that the advantaged one won't be able to find because they weren't pushed to find it because they weren't disadvantaged. The advantaged one's strength comes from having the advantage, while the disadvantaged one's strength comes from the unknown; creativity is the strongest advantage in any duel. Therefore, the disadvantaged one only remains disadvantaged if they fail to utilize the strongest advantage, creativity.

Wanting Without Need (Indonesian):

Ketika kita mendapatkan apa yang kita paling ingin, namun, kita tidak murni hatinya mengapa kita membutuhkannya, apa yang dimaksudkan untuk terjadi tidak terjadi karena sumber kemurnian penting disediakan oleh alam semesta bukan ... Kemurnian adalah apa yang dimaksudkan untuk diungkapkan, dan jika salah satu tidak memberikan kemurnian dari hati sendiri, alam semesta akan memberikan kemurnian yang satu gagal untuk menunjukkan untuk mengajar satu untuk menjadi murni dengan kebutuhan seseorang untuk apa yang paling ingin; Sayangnya, beberapa diajarkan pelajaran ini sulit untuk kematian mereka ... Oleh karena itu menjadi contoh bagi yang lain ketika seseorang gagal untuk belajar pelajaran keras yang ingin tanpa murni perlu mirip dengan menjadi haus dan mengabaikan salah satu yang memuaskan dahaga tersebut dengan minum dari sumur beracun.

Translated to English:
When we get what we most want, yet, we are not pure at heart at why we need it, what is meant to happen does not happen because the source of the vital purity is provided by the Universe instead... Purity is what is meant to be expressed, and if one is not providing the purity from one's own heart, the Universe will provide the purity that one fails to show in order to teach one to be pure with one's need for what one most wants. Unfortunately, some are taught this hard lesson to their demise... Therefore becoming an example to others of when someone fails to learn the hard lesson that wanting without a pure needing is akin to being thirsty and ignoring that one is quenching such thirst by drinking from a poisonous well.

Be A Futurian (Romanian):

Ei spun că cei care nu învață din trecut, sunt sortite să-l repet ... dar eu spun, cei care învață doar din trecut, de asemenea, sortită Se repetă ... Unul Ori trăiește istorie sau Predă Istoria ... devine un exemplu viu al unui istoric și cel mai bine la doar o altă parte a istoriei ... Numai cei care știu și de a face ceea ce Istoria nu poate învăța cu adevărat trăiesc pe dincolo de istorie, ele sunt cele ale viitorului ...

Translated to English:
They say that those who do not learn from the past are doomed to repeat it. But I say, those who only learn from the past are also doomed to repeat it. One either lives out history or teaches history... Becomes a living example of an historian and at best just another part of history. Only those who know and do what history can never teach truly live on beyond history, they are the Futurians...

The Greatest Deception (Haitian Creole):

Desepsyon nan pi gran se yon avètisman pwofetik ki desepsyon lan pi gran se toujou ap vini yo nan lòd yo twonpe moun ap tann pou yon gwo desepsyon vini nan kwè yo ke yo pa te deja te twonpe tèt nou pa desepsyon nan pi gran.
- Soti nan liv **la inevitab la kont destine**

Translated to English:
The Greatest Deception is a prophetic warning that the Greatest Deception is Still to Come in order to Deceive those waiting for a coming Great Deception into believing that they haven't already been deceived by The Greatest Deception.
--from the book **The Inevitable Versus Destiny**

Revolve or Advance (Spanish):

En general, la llamada para el cambio de las masas se deriva de un estado de aburrimiento de los que en el escenario. Y por lo general cuando los actores son reemplazadas y el guión se rehashed prometer la misma recompensa no se puede entregar la alegría de masas y aplauden la vieja demostración hizo de nuevo una vez más. El asentamiento de equivalencia sobre la excelencia es la clave a la esclavitud. Revolución le dice exactamente y, literalmente, lo que es, las masas giran alrededor del mismo agujero negro vacío de la sociedad sobre-exagerar una sobrevaloración del bajo rendimiento. No es una cuestión de ser repugnante con el fin de cambiar el mundo, es una cuestión de la introducción de un nuevo mundo y acogedor, y abrazando a los que entran con usted.

Translated to English:

Generally the call for change from the masses derives from a state of boredom at those on the stage... And usually when the actors are replaced and the script is rehashed to promise the same undeliverable reward the masses cheer and applaud the old show made anew once again. The settling for equivalence over excellence is the key to enslavement. Revolution tells you exactly and literally what it is, the masses revolve around the same empty black hole of societal over-hyping an overvaluing of underachievement. It's not a matter of being revolting in order to change the world, it is a matter of introducing a new world and welcoming and embracing those who enter it with you.

Altering The World (Catalan):

Un no pot canviar el món sense ira, que és l'arrel del canvi, és a dir. "Ange"; a continuació, però, un món canviat per la ira és un món nascut de la ira i un món nascut de la ira només pot seguir sent vital com un món, sempre que els combustibles originals còlera que ... un cop que aquesta ira desapareix i totes les seves ramificacions ja no motivar , generalment una nova generació enutjat canviarà el món de nou ... la creació d'un cercle viciós d'un any d'edat ira a la següent. En lloc de canviar el món, oferir un món alternatiu. Això es pot fer amb l'amor, la lògica i la llum on la ira no ha de jugar un paper.

Translated to English:

One cannot change the World without anger, which is the root of Change, ie. "ange"; yet, a World changed by anger is a World then born of anger and a World born of anger can only remain vital as a World as long as the original anger fuels it... Once such anger subsides and all of its offshoots no longer motivate, usually a new angry generation will change the World again... setting up a vicious cycle of one angry age to the next. Rather than changing the World, offer an Alternative World. This can be done with love, logic and light where anger need not play a role.

True Leadership Leads The Unwilling (Latin):

Ductus nec volunt facere ut populum facere, aut dux partim ex animo. Ut populum ductus est tamen nolunt facere melius faciet populum. In causa est differentia gradus afflatu gaudent ... quid facere velle, frui invitum dicere quam facere nolint, sed usquam. Quod est verum ductu.

Leadership is not getting the people to do what they want to do, such is either a Coach or Cheerleader. Leadership is getting the people to do what they don't want to do yet must do for the betterment of the people. It is the difference in the levels of inspiration and motivation... The willing enjoy being told what to do, the unwilling enjoy telling you how they don't want to do it, but do it anyway. That's true leadership.

The Exceptional Exception
English:
There is an exception to every rule, except for this rule that has no exception. Therefore not every rule has an exception. Except this is the exception to the rule that there are exceptions to every rule. Therefore this is an exception to a rule and a rule which has no exceptions.

Translated to Welsh:
Mae yna eithriad i bob rheol, ac eithrio ar gyfer y rheol hon sydd heb eithriad. Felly, nid oes gan bob rheol eithriad. Heblaw hyn yw'r eithriad i'r rheol bod yna eithriadau i'r rheol bob. Felly mae hyn yn eithriad i'r rheol a rheol sydd heb unrhyw eithriadau.

Other Stories Inspired and Written During the Writing of This Version of Adah and The Great Seven

0) (Preface) The Eagle And The Wren- *The inspiration for this story came forth from our discussion of the role of the Eagles and Falcons in the Adah story, and how the Eagle is the sole bird which flies above the storm. We thought, what would happen if another bird surprisingly found itself above the storm with the Eagle and how would this bird respond to a place of peace when there is so much turmoil for her fellow peers in the storm below? We borrowed from an old favorite legend of the Wren, the Kinglet, and off we went in an unexpected direction, especially for the Eagle.*

1) The Ocean, The Shore And The Mountains- *Since this version of Adah and the Great Seven is expanded from the movie Holy Galileo!, we decided to do the same to a major theme in the movie, which is how the Ocean and the Shore more deeply relate beyond the superficial cliché of Shores drawing in waves and the Ocean leaving behind water-logged gifts. What we found in this expansion surprised us because we went far beyond a call to powerfully unite into a deeper understanding of how forces of the temporary and the eternal collaborate to produce an understanding beyond discord and harmony. Those that seek harmony between the temporary and the* eternal are really trying to stop the natural flow of the Universe. Harmony can only be found when the temporary and eternal collaborate.

2) **The Monarch: Arriving Is Leaving-** We wrote this story near the end of this book when we were looking for a couple of final captions to the title pages of each part. Yes, these stories were once a lot shorter and some even just a mere few passages conveying a major point or two; yet, as we kept editing and reformatting, we kept adding on to each story until they all just became too long to fit our original format. This story was originally just a collection of three maxims and a couple of loose couplings between each... A Monarch Butterfly landed on our window and the rest is history, or, as in your case, the future.

3) **Swallows, Sparrows And Song-** This is the last piece written for this book. As much as we would like to say the characters depicted in the story bear no resemblance to anyone in public life, such is not the case. We confess now Harold is based on the happy-go-lucky wunderkind Harry Styles and Malena, the sultry siren Selena Gomez. Yet the purpose of this story is to reintroduce a quest that humanity has completely overlooked as necessary, perhaps even vital in the understanding of ourselves. How does one use music to enlighten the world?

4) **God Declares As The Devil Tells-** As we wrote this piece, we were literally writing from beyond ourselves. We would laugh out loud as we finished and reread each stanza. This piece of writing may always mean a lot more to us than anyone else, and that is fine with us. If it comes close to meaning as much within you as it does to us, then you my brother or sister will have comprehended a truth of truths concerning Us, the Universe and how All relates to All.

The Ocean, the Shore and the Mountains
(Prelude to the Mountains of Oceania)

**It's not so much that the Shore draws in the waves,
it's that the waves
are turning the Mountains into Shoreline.
---from the movie "Holy Galileo!"**

The Ocean declared triumphantly to the Mountains,
"In time I will turn you all into Shoreline."

The Mountains scoffed,
"What? One grain of sand at a time? Spare us your warning. The quickest you could be done is at least a million years from now, and for some of us a hundred million or more."

The Ocean stoically replied,
"Oh dear Mountains, you forget I was here long before you ever shot up from the earth in a blaze of balling glory yelling and screaming your own measurements of eternity... And I will be here even longer than that after I am done with you. For to you, a million to a hundred million years seems like eternity. But for me, a million years is as long and is as short as I want it to be, for I am eternal."

The Mountains defiantly replied,
"You may turn us into dust, yet another group of us will rise and tower over you."

The Ocean sternly reminded the mountains,
"If need be, I will bury you all again, like I presently do the Mid-Ocean Range, the longest attempt by you to express your superiority over me yet remains underneath my dominance. Consider it an honor that I slowly turn you into the Shore and allow your temporary time as a majestic outcropping of unnecessary brute force to exist in my presence."

The Mountains laughed,
"Why do you hate the temporary so much?"

The Ocean laughed,
"The same could be asked of your disrespectful disregard for the eternal."

They both stood in silence rather than answer.
The Mountain peaked while the Ocean waved.

The impasse between the temporary Mountains and the eternal Ocean would normally result in a slow passing of time one grain of sand after another like in an hour glass as tall as the moon above the earth; except the actual grains of sand known as the Shore offered up itself as a haven of understanding between the Mountains and the Ocean as it often does for vacationers looking for a little fun in the sun.

"Look and listen you two, I'm as part of one of you as I am the other. My grains are the result of when the temporary becomes the eternal, and my flatness demonstrates how the eternal can be reshifted into temporary shapes. So I can see more than anyone how both of you are necessary to each other and for each other. Neither of you are more important in the creation of me. Therefore, both of you, the temporary and the eternal, the Mountains and the Ocean, the supplier of my being and the essence of my doing are one in purpose."

The Ocean and the Mountains ignored this call to maturity from the Shore.

The Ocean roared,
"I could send tidal wave after tidal wave!"

And the Mountains bellowed,

"I could erupt and erupt into a chain of new volcanoes!"

The Shore with grace and dignity hushed the cacophony of their misunderstanding of who and what each were to each other. Such a silence had never been heard so loudly.

"You can't be what you can only make and you can't make until you be unmade. Nothing temporary can be made eternal, and nothing eternal can be made temporary. Both simply must be unmade in order to make the present feel like now, rather than just a fleeting moment which passes too quickly or an elongated passage of time that feels like one is crawling in a tunnel through the center of the earth. The eternal can't speed up the temporary and the temporary can't slow down the eternal. I will be made as I am meant to be made in the due time appropriated for the both of you. Now act accordingly."

The Ocean and the Mountains for the first time peacefully sighed.

The Shore took advantage of the lull their resignation provided for one last hurrah of enlightenment.
"What did you expect when you the Mountains, the temporary, and you the Ocean, the eternal, merged? Did you imagine you would become anything else other than me? I am the greatness of both of you. So let yourself be content that you end up becoming me when you both know you could never end up being me without the other... You're not in opposition, you are **in** position to become greater than you ever could on your own."

The Mountains rejoiced in now knowing that the Shore did not represent their demise by the Ocean... And the Ocean celebrated that the Shore represented them in a partnership rather than a conquering by a conqueror. For, no one likes to be told that their destiny ends in their decimation or they must continue to conquer relentlessly without the freedom to cooperate or show mercy.

The Shore offered the Mountains an everlasting hereafter, a peaceful being, and the Ocean a liberation to be more than just a conqueror, a creator of peace.

The Mountains grateful for the elevated understanding now between themselves and the Ocean asked for such understanding of another opponent,
"What pray tell of the Wind?"

The Shore then taught the Mountains that the Wind is nothing more than a lighter Ocean merging with them to create the Desert.
The Mountains became even more grateful.

All elevated understanding comes from the merger of oppositions becoming partnerships.

Presently, are you trying to be
as tall and majestic as a Mountain,
or as relentless and exalted as the Ocean?
Instead of being one opposing the other,
be as the Shore which provides a place for
what is temporary about you to
work in tandem and in harmony with
all that is eternal within you.

The Monarchs: Arriving Is Leaving

As the millions of Monarchs arrived at Parícutin for the winter, two of them were engaged in a unique discourse between a Master and Apprentice.

The Apprentice, "How good does it feel to have finally arrived?"

The Master, "Arriving is leaving."

The Apprentice, "Not when we have just arrived."

The Master, "Especially when we have just arrived."

The Apprentice, "Look, we just flew a thousand plus miles from San Juan Capistrano to be here, the last thing on my mind after such a long journey is leaving again."

The Master, "It's not meant to be the first thing or the last thing on your mind. It is simply meant to be as on your mind as is arriving."

The Apprentice, "Why? We are not leaving for months. I will worry about it when the time for leaving gets closer."

The Master, "If you're not prepared to leave this instant, then you won't be prepared when you think the time is closer."

The Apprentice, "How could I possibly be prepared to leave this instant, when I just got here?"

The Master, "That is because one of us wasted their time pretending they were on a journey to arrive here, while the other one of us took advantage of that time to prepare themselves that they could leave here the instant they arrived here."

The Apprentice, "Sounds like one of us took time to enjoy the journey, and can now enjoy this destination, and the other is too busy arriving before one has arrived so one can be leaving while one is staying..."

The Master, "The reality is this, we will be leaving in a few months, so preparing to leave can begin at any time since leaving is part of our reality."

The Apprentice, "Maybe I won't leave. Maybe I'll just stay here."

The Master, "Deciding to stay is to journey in a different way than the rest of the Monarchs. You are then leaving by prolonging your arrival."

The Apprentice, "Why can't anything just be what it is without you making it into something else, especially its opposite?"

The Master, "Because the essence of arrival and leaving is purely your perspective of what and how you think you are relating to the world. The moment you say you are arriving, you bring with it the definition that you could also be leaving. Therefore, you are doing both each and every time you use either definition."

The Apprentice, "So you are saying that I am the one who is making something different out of what actually is, and therefore introducing the opposite of what and where I am actually being."

The Master, "Yes, we are always here, during the so-called journey we are here, during the so-called arrival we are here. As we leave, we are here; and as we journey again, we are here. Yet, we are experiencing being here in different ways. The experiences do not alter that we are here, no matter how hard we might try to convince ourselves otherwise."

The Apprentice, "So you're saying I can't arrive here any more than I was already here while I was on my way to arrive here."

The Master, "You were not able to experience this place as here until you arrived here, but now that you're here, you will not fully be here until you also see that this place is preparing you for the next place for you to experience truly being here. In essence, arriving is leaving. For this experience of being here is as welcoming as much as saying goodbye to you being where you are meant to be to fully experience being here."

The Apprentice, "So what you're saying to me is no arrival or leaving is permanent, it is a constant motion between the two no matter where you are."

The Master, "Yes, in reality you are always here and always remain here no matter how much arriving and leaving you do. Yet, the concept of arriving and leaving can serve a purpose as long as that concept serves you rather than you become a servant of it."

The Apprentice, "So, you're saying that as we traveled here from San Juan Capistrano that each time we stopped to rest along the way we were arriving as much as we were leaving that spot."

The Master, "Yes, very much so. The leaving from that spot was obvious, and everything we did while there was to prepare us to leave there. Yet, we had also just as much arrived, and if any of us had decided to stay there, and not leave, such a possibility was also available to any of us."

The Apprentice, "All of us knew we weren't going to stay the moment we got there."

The Master, "Yes, true, yet it is the Master who knows that one can be compelled to stay as much as leave from anywhere, because one is always grounded that one is here no matter where they experience it."

The Apprentice, "Why do we leave and then arrive and then leave again in the first place?"

The Master, "The real question is this... Why do we call what we were doing arriving and leaving, when all that we are ever really doing is creating and manifesting all the time everywhere we go?"

The Apprentice, "So, now I'm not even arriving or leaving anymore?"

The Master, "You still are. You are just beginning to see that the description of yourself arriving and leaving is nothing more than a tool for you to adjust your creative and manifestation process rather than being your full disclosure on what you are actually doing when you arrive and leave."

The Apprentice, "So, I am either arriving or leaving, or somehow I'm *doing both at the same time. Then I'm not really arriving and leaving because I'm always here no matter how I might otherwise describe it, and yet again, I am arriving and leaving so that I can attune myself to being here when I might be out of tune of that, due to me either doing more leaving or arriving without an acknowledgment of the other at the same time."*

The Master, "It appears that our lesson is done for the day. Let us now enjoy our arrival as we begin to prepare for our departure."

The Apprentice, "Yeah, because that departure could be as early as tomorrow morning."

The Master, "It is."

The Apprentice, "What?! I haven't even unpacked yet!"

The Master, "Sounds like you're already prepared."

The Apprentice, "Where could we possible go that would be a better fit for us than right here, right now?"

The Master, "No place is a perfect fit until you realize that any place is a perfect fit for you to arrive at and leave from."

The Apprentice, "Are we leaving tomorrow morning just so you can prove this point to me?"

The Master, "We would have left tomorrow morning if that point had not already been proven to you."

The Apprentice, "Dear Master, I cannot deny the greatness of your teaching."

The Master, "Dear Apprentice, no, what cannot be denied is the greatness of your learning. No teacher can teach unless the student learns. For the student can learn even if the teacher is unable to teach."

The Apprentice, "What could the student possibly learn that the teacher cannot teach?"

The Master, "How to teach, if the student is truly there to learn what is being taught."

The Apprentice, "I see that I have only been watching and looking at what we've been doing as we arrive and leave, rather than observing and perceiving that we are doing more while at the same time doing less than arriving and leaving, and being shortsighted as such, I am only able to be here partially even as I feel as though I am fully here, because I keep referring to my movement as arriving or leaving."

The Master, "How would you describe your movement otherwise?"

The Apprentice, "That's just it, if I'm going to describe it, this is one way and perhaps the best way to describe movement. Yet, I realize no matter how well I am able to describe it as movement, such is only a description and not what I'm actually doing."

The Master, "What are you actually doing?"

The Apprentice, "I am learning how to describe."

The Master, "Then you must also realize that the terms teaching and learning are merely descriptions of us describing what is happening here, and is not what is actually happening here."

The Apprentice, "If teaching and learning is not what we're actually doing here, then what are we doing?"

The Master, "We are showing each other that there is another who can show us the possibility that we can be shown."

The Apprentice, "So beyond the teaching and the learning are two beings who are doing more than simply showing each other that they can show each other, they are showing the other that they too can show there are things which can be shown beyond themselves."

The Master, "Yes, in that process of showing to each other, we use the terms teaching and learning to describe a certain way that we show. When you recognize that all that you're doing is showing and being shown, that is the best that any amount of teaching and learning can ever do. So the description falls short of what one is actually doing. Yet, at the same time the description can describe a place where such showing is the focus of one's actions. Whereas one is showing and being shown just as much indirectly that one would not describe as a teaching and learning scenario."

The Apprentice, "In other words, teaching and learning is just a description for when someone shows them something and the other shows they are being shown that something by the other. What is really going on when we describe teaching and learning can be summed up in this statement, let me show you something, and then you show me I was able to show you."

The Master, "Yes, now you're catching on. There is a world whereby we describe and live within those descriptions, and then there is the world we actually live in and do things beyond anything we can describe. When one tries to make the descriptive world the actual world, and forgo the actual world they live in, one is always waiting for something to happen first so they can then give it a definitive description so they can therefore properly wait for the next thing to happen which they will also describe afterward."

The Apprentice, "Action derives only from the world beyond description."

The Master, "For instance, reading and writing are descriptions of what is presently happening here. Yet, such is not what is actually happening."

The Apprentice, "Are you about to tell the reader that they are not actually reading this book as they are reading this book?"

The Master, "No, I don't have to tell them what they already know. Describing what they are presently doing as reading a book falls well short of the reality of what they are actually doing, because one could read a cookbook but not actually be doing what the cookbook shows is there to be done unless one is also presently cooking."

The Apprentice, "What exactly are they supposed to be cooking as they read this?"

The Master, "That they are about to be shown something that the world has never been shown before, and they must be able to show that such has been shown to them."

The Apprentice nodded and the first item he unpacked was a cookbook on preparing a feast.

Do you consider that you are now just reading a book like you do any other book, and as a reader of this book, you will one day stop reading this book whether you read the entire book or not, and simply move on to the next book like you did all the other books you read before you read this book? Or do you truly realize you are being shown something which the world has never been shown and therefore trying to describe what you are now doing as just reading another book falls well short of what is actually happening here, which is you are participating in a real-time live discovery of one of if not the greatest ideas ever to grace our awareness? Yes, you may close the covers and put this book down one day, yet, what is happening here, what really is happening here, beyond you reading a book is something you will never experience in this way again. You can either live only in the world of your descriptions and let others know that you read this book or you can join us in an awareness of what is actually happening here, which is, we are showing we can be shown we can be as great as the ideas we think are great.

Authors' Note – This is the original sketch of this story. We are currently working on a full version plus a movie treatment to be made into a film. Also, One Direction fans, happy Easter Egg hunting.

Swallows, Sparrows And Song

Long before there were any humans, singing and making music, long before there were any bugs clicking and chirping bug-like sounds, long before there were frogs ribbitting and croaking, and long before there were any other animals, roaring and howling through the night, there were the birds perfecting singing and song. If you look up the origin of music you'll find a blurb about Zeus and the nine muses or some other fantastical explanation, when in reality the birds invented and reinvented music many times over to their own pleasure and purposes. This is the story of one of those inventions... Some say it is the story of their last invention. For the pleasure and purpose they found was unlike any they had ever found before, and they haven't been able to top it ever since.

Each year a competition is held for which group of birds shall be the group to sing the song of songs for all the birds to enjoy and sing along in order to offer an opportunity at world peace.

The competition now known as "Who's Got It?!" was once called "In Search of Unification". Everyone at one time believed that the key to a civilized, peaceful society was determined by the structure and melody of a song. Even one of the smartest of the humans, Socrates, was taught this is true by his music teacher, Damon.

The motto of the competition was "Finding the Song finds the Peace."

Those romantic days of higher aspirations for the competition have long since passed. These days it's nothing more than a giant money grab on how to sell the ideas of peace and harmonization through the music business. The other birds who do not win are sold on how to sing along so that they can appear to be peaceful (rather than showing how peaceful they are by singing along in celebration to the winning song), because none of the winning songs are ever allowed to cut deep enough into any bird's core for there to be any real movement of world peace.

The leaders recognized the necessity of the facade that the competition offered long ago, and minimized what could be done through the competition. That is why it always came down to two groups of birds, the Swallows and the Sparrows.

And once again, this year the two groups competing head-to-head in the finals are the Swallows and the Sparrows. That is because it was deemed by the social engineers who work for the leaders that the Swallows and Sparrows were both wonderfully melodic yet offered no real threat of subversive thoughts and ideas. They were considered the most conforming and compliant singers in the bird kingdom.

At least that is what they figured was true... Here is what happened when a Swallow and a Sparrow realized the fix was in and they formulated a way out after they were forced out and had to conform and comply on a way back in to force everyone out as well.

Something strange was already in the air because the winners had been either a Sparrow or a Swallow for a century or more except for last year. Both were so good, the judges considered a tie between them. Neither side was satisfied with that result, so they vowed to never let that happen again. Well, they vowed never to lose again, and sharing the top honor just meant they both lost, not both won. Also, having the birds sing along as either a

Swallow or a Sparrow where there was no clear winner between the two gave birth to the two party system in each and every political realm.

The leaders felt a need to control the outcome and implemented tiebreakers so that a tie would never happen again. The actual tiebreaker process would be kept secret from the masses so if need be, the leaders could pacify them and console them that a certain songbird was so close to winning but would not be allowed to win simply because they were not the choice of the leaders.

No one could have expected what happened, especially the leaders, when everything changed... When the greatest song ever heard was sung... And then unsung... And then sung by everyone...

Everyone felt that this year was different, and not just because there was a determination to have only one Champion, there was an heightened sense of quality in the air... These really were the best of the best the competition had seen in years...

Regardless that each group of birds had sent the best from each group in years, the two finalists were a Swallow and a Sparrow. Anticipation was high, because either the Sparrow and the Swallow would rise to the occasion and trump the best from the field, or there would be a gigantic upset not seen since a nightingale won the competition over a century ago.

The Sparrow, a young lad from the Isle of Man, sang what some would consider one of the greatest songs of all time, well if not the greatest, perhaps the best song ever. He knew he sang the perfect song to perfection, and yet he thought to himself, "The story of my life did not show any magic upon my audience." In fact, he was the only contestant that received no applause, just stunned silence and he surely expected more than this... It was as if he had ventured into another world and he had been thrown to

the wolves. One thing he learned from his 18 trainers and his favorite teacher, Diana, he said to himself "No poor reception is gonna drag me down." So, with heavy clouds of doubt now hanging over him, he no longer had a temporary fix for the little things, and he murmured to himself,
"Where do broken hearts go?"

Unbeknownst to Harold, a Raven, an enchantress, was all too pleased with herself with Harold's ineptitude to transfix the audience.

The Swallow, a young chica from the mid-west plains of the Continental Territories, did not hear the Sparrow sing but most certainly noticed that something had gone awry with the performance. The audience appeared restless, as if lost in a cave without a guide or light to help them escape. She told herself to stay focused, be solid, and the competition would be hers. Then she sang. What she heard was the most beautiful rendition of her song she had ever performed, and that normally would have pleased her to no end because the crown would not be denied from such a performance. There was only one problem. She recognized it wasn't her song. Yes, the words were the words written by her, but the voice which sang those words was not her voice. That voice belonged to the one who now rushed toward her on the stage.

The Sparrow, named Harold, confronted the Swallow, "Olivia, what are you doing, and don't tell me a lie either."

She corrected him, "Olivia is my twin sister. I am Malena, and you being out here is totally against protocol."

Before Harold could respond, the crowd erupted into loud jeers, "Fool's Gold!!!"

The Loud Speaker commanded that the audience calm down and

allow the judges to sort out these shenanigans.

The Head Judge, "God only knows why the two of you have pulled this stunt, were you up all night concocting this grand illusion? Because nothing will save you tonight unless you stand up right now and show you will not make the same mistakes that you just did. Don't forget where you belong, because at the end of the day, you might consider yourself forever young, but you will be history and no longer fireproof as you tumble the long way down through the dark spaces of irrelevance."

Harold and Malena were told to sing their parts over again, yet, this time, sing each in their own voice.

Harold stepped up first, and unprecedented, Malena was allowed to listen as he sang. As soon as he began, Malena's astonishment equaled her anger. She cut him off before he finished the first verse, "Why are you singing like a Swallow, and not just any Swallow, like me?"

Harold had no real answer but felt a wave of emotion come over him, "I want... I wish... I would... I should've kissed you!"

Malena, aghast, "You should have what?!"

Before Harold could respond, the judges had him removed from the stage and disqualified from the competition.

The Swallows in the audience actually booed his removal, yet, his own kind, the Sparrows, were overjoyed that the traitor would see the stage no more, yelling out, "Na Na Na!" until Harold could be seen no more.

Harold, perplexed, pondered why he had no control over his voice.

The Head Judge turned to Malena, "Now, before I change my mind and change your ticket to be on this show to no entry, you must sing your song in your own voice or risk ruining everything about you."

Malena, nervous, adjusted her little black dress, then began singing her song in Harold's voice all over again. The Sparrows erupted in applause, while the Swallows booed.

Malena yelled at her fellow Swallows. "C'mon c'mon, I want to write you a song if you'll stop trying to have a heart attack!" The Swallows booed louder. Malena yelled louder. "You don't realize how strong I am. I am not ready to run!"

A certain Swallow hollered above the rest. "She's not afraid to be taken as something great!"

The mass of Swallows began beckoning her to join them. The Swallows alarmed yelled, "You can't steal my girl!"

A leader of the Swallows hollered back, "Why not?! She stole my heart!"

At this moment the judges felt a bit of Stockholm Syndrome seeping in as if they were going to side with the Sparrows or the Swallows for the admiration or disdain for Malena. "It's time for you to go home."

Malena. "I have half a heart to go with the Sparrows because life is too short not to live while we're young." So then Malena turned to the Swallows, started to blow a kiss and turn and patted her bum and yelled to them, "Love you, Goodbye!"

The Swallows in mock desperation hollered, "Don't forget we loved you first! But we refuse to come back for you until infinity no matter how irresistible you can be."

Harold, watching backstage as Malena was escorted past him said to her, "Girl Almighty, does he know what happened?" He, being Jaque Azzizoff, their manager, a surly pigeon that talked like an Eagle, but cut deals like a Southern Cassowary.

Malena, "He probably thinks that I refuse to act my age."

Harold, "That you are moments away from becoming a Sparrow."

Malena, "I've never felt more alive. If I could fly, I would happily kiss you."

Harold suddenly truly, madly, deeply and boldly in love proclaimed, "That would most definitely be my last first kiss!"

Malena grew concerned that Harold might spill the secret of their summer love, "You and I, they don't know about us."

Harold laughed because Harold knows a secret relationship between him and Malena is never enough to satisfy either one of them, "That's what makes you beautiful, nobody compares to us."

Malena, "What a feeling, our midnight memories as the night changes into dawn while you rock me with sweet little white lies of why we don't go there for real."

Harold, "Hey angel face, do you know what has happened to us?"

Malena, "No, I don't, but one way or another we are going to find out."

Harold, "Perhaps you misused your witchy stuff."

Malena, "Oh yeah, perhaps you misused your wizardry stuff."

A raven could be heard snickering in the far corner.

Harold, "Me? It's gotta be you!"

Malena, "You would think that if you were only wishing on a star and not dealing with reality."

Harold, "No matter, you're still the one for me."

Malena, "Do they know it's Christmas?"

Harold, "What are you talking about?" Harold knew damn well what he was talking about. Such was code between them on whether someone else was in on their secret plan to reveal and implement the purpose associated with the origin of music.

Malena realized the answer to that question and tried to cover up her intention, "That's how confused my brain feels when you say that to me."

And with that, the colossal break-up of the relationship that no one knew about but now did and therefore opened the flood gates of lamentations and distress over a union that had already been vaporized. Everyone was now sad that they broke up even though they never knew they were together. Yet, still a secret to all, was the origin of music, which appeared would remain a secret forevermore, much to the delight of a certain raven who used the power and authority of the origin of music all to and for herself.

Harold, now shunned by the Sparrows, found a claim with the Swallows because he now sang in a prettier voice than any Swallow had ever sung. Likewise, Malena was embraced by the Sparrows after being discarded by the Swallows for she could bellow better than any Sparrow ever sang.

Both achieved a status beyond what any songbirds had ever achieved. There were Team Harold and Team Malena apparel selling out. Radio stations would exclusively play only one or the other. The entire bird population was divided over a Sparrow who seemed more Swallow and a Swallow who seemed more Sparrow and since the competition declared that there would be no winner,
due to what they considered a shamockery by these two, the world chose a de facto champion anyway.

Without a true champion, chaos began to unravel the fringes of the fabric of society. Birds turned against birds in unruly ways rarely seen before. A new term was coined for such bad and mindless behavior, from what sounded like a deep guttural roaring from their beaks, that term is "war".

The two did try to reconcile their relationship and take control of this divide in a secret rendezvous. Harold informed Malena that since she is not actually a Sparrow but only a Swallow, she should give up singing in order to be with him and return to their original plan to reveal the origin of music. Malena informed Harold back that since he was not a Swallow, but a Sparrow, that he should give up singing to be with her and then they could return to their plan to reveal the origin of music. Both proclaimed to the other that they were born to sing and that not to sing even if they didn't sing like themselves would be robbing them of their birthright. No love is worth forsaking one's destiny, and no destiny is worth forsaking for a cause dependent upon the acceptance of others. So they parted and returned to an atmosphere of overwhelming acclaim from those who had adopted them.

Until the rebellious hype-bubble burst with the ruling by the competition committee it read:

'After further investigating, the two outlaws who perpetrated a charade of preposterous maneuverings that neither could sing in their own voice, but rather sang in the voice of the other, we hereby, therefore, frankly and without a doubt henceforth, bygones are banishing not only these two charlatan heroes who took advantage of a once in a lifetime opportunity to lead the public astray from the seriousness of finding the best song sung by the best singer. Without further adieu, we are announcing the eternal banishment of all Sparrows and Swallows from the competition, forevermore, on and on and to infinity.'

In an effort to appease the ruling committee, the Sparrows and Swallows immediately exiled Harold and Malena, burned every record and deleted every file which mentioned them or their songs.

The ruling committee granted a public hearing for the Sparrows and Swallows to make their case to be allowed back in to the competition. While the Sparrows and Swallows got to work on making their case in the best possible light, the rest of the birds were secretly hoping that the ruling committee would stick to its harsh verdict, and never allow them in the competition again. They feigned and prawned about how disrespectful the Swallows and Sparrows had been as the reason why they were so dead-set on their exclusion, yet the truth is they just wanted a better chance to win. Meanwhile, Harold and Malena, having gone from young prodigy to public shaming to bizarre star status and now total irreverence found life out of the public eye a refreshing lifestyle blessing that they would have never known they would enjoy so much if they had not been exiled. They never became a couple again. They simply shared a state of being that no one else in the world shared with them. They still enjoyed singing, and now without the pressures of the world using them as a prop of their own inner divisions, the two found they enjoyed singing duets more than they ever did singing on their own.

At 3 each day, that is 3 A.M., by the way, not 3 P.M., they would meet up and sing together whatever they were feeling or thinking or vibing or loving or whatever and usually they would sing until the dawn because that is the quietest time to hear themselves before the world awakens and rushes about drowning out any songs not on the public list to broadcast.

No other birds could hear them because they were located in a region where sound did not carry beyond a few feet beyond themselves. They didn't care that no one could hear them, to the point they didn't feel the world deserved to hear them after tossing them aside into the wasteland. They also didn't care or felt the world deserved to know the secret of the origin of music. Of course, as with any edict, not all of the birds obeyed and stayed away from the couple. A certain parrot known as Ed, would at 2:55 find a spot near enough to Harold and Malena to listen to them sing. Now you might think the parrot did this with a benign motivation of just wanting to hear the beautiful music Harold and Malena shared with each other, except this parrot was born with a heart of sinister silver. Ed, being a parrot, began to parrot the best song, which hinted at the origin of music in its rhythm, that Harold and Malena had ever written together. Each morning, as the sun rose up from the horizon, they would close out their singing ceremony with this remarkable tribute song to love, life and resurgence.

Three months later, on the eve of the first competition since the Harold and Malena fiasco, the parrot felt comfortable enough to perform their song that the parrot knew no one else in the world had ever heard.

When Ed, being a parrot, was able to parrot the two different voices as if they were one, the judges halted the competition right on the spot and declared the parrot the winner with barely over ten percent of the performers having performed. The song and the parrot's rendition became so overwhelmingly popular that many

considered it the greatest song of all time.
When asked how could it be possible that a parrot could write something original and the first thing ever written is critically acclaimed as the greatest song ever written, how did the parrot do it? The parrot responded, "Well, as you know, we parrots, have been both cursed and blessed with the ability to mimic any singer or song no matter how bad or good that song is, and are proud members of the historical society, yet what many of you do not realize is, underneath all this repetition is a proud voice ready to show the world that we parrots can more than hold our own with any songbird."

The parrot was asked, "Do you think you would have beaten any Sparrow or Swallow contestant if they would have been allowed to compete?"

'That's funny,' thought a certain toucan, Harv, 'because to me that parrot's voice sounds very similar to a certain Sparrow and Swallow that the general public has already deleted from their awareness.' Being a private investigator, this toucan was already suspicious how easily the public bought and the parrot sold this story of miraculous originality. So, he decided that he would break the edict to stay away from Harold and Malena, and inquire if Ed had paid them a visit or not, because, the toucan thought, 'what a great way to recrank the competition again by having a parrot mimic your song to win the championship.' If that was the case, the toucan wanted to congratulate them on a job well done before he exposed them for major financial gain to the world. As Ed's popularity reached global status pressure began to mount for a follow-up song. Yet, with all the attention on Ed and his whereabouts, he wasn't free enough to sneak away and spy on Harold and Malena again to nick a new song. So Ed hired a crew from the underground, the mockingbirds to spy for him, and steal an album's worth of material from Harold and Malena.
The mockingbirds readily agreed and that evening flew off with a devious plan of the their own to hear what Harold and Malena

were singing .

Harv, the toucan, was surprised to see the arrival of six mockingbirds at the exiled location of Harold and Malena, he had expected Ed the parrot to show up. He thought to himself, 'They must be here on his behalf.' So, Harv put off talking to Harold and Malena to observe what would go down. The mockingbirds stayed for a week and never once spoke to Harold and Malena. Harv knew then they were up to no good.

Ed the parrot didn't know how much no good they were really up to.

When the mockingbirds returned, only one greeted Ed to teach him the new song they had heard coming from Harold and Malena. Ed, being a parrot, couldn't tell if the song was good or not, but figuring it came from Harold and Malena, he felt secure that it would impress the judges enough for him to get past the first round and therefore establish himself as a legitimate songbird.

So, when Ed stepped up to sing his new song, the anticipation in the audience had never been higher for an artist. By the time Ed hit the eighth note, birds were screeching and heading for the exits yelling "This is the most abominable noise we have ever heard!!! Ed is a sham!"

Unbeknownst to Ed, the mockingbird had taught him the song of vultures as they gobbled down on dead carcasses. Ed, the parrot, was ruined as an artist. With half the audience gone, the lights grew dim and then shot on again hot, bright white... And five mockingbirds appeared on the stage, as the newest, hottest, freshest, sexiest, tastiest, rawest, boldest, boy band to hit the stage since Many Erections last performed during their "Who Needs a Pinky Anyway?" World Tour, and when they hit that first note of their song, the crowd couldn't run fast enough back into the arena. Everyone was pleased except for two birds: Ed, The parrot, who realized he had been outscammed in his own scam, and Harv, the toucan who now had to shift his blackmail scheme toward the most despicable species because they would just slit his throat rather than pay any ransom. Those five cherubs on the stage may prance and dance and sing and swoon like angelic dogooders from 50s style sitcoms but underneath that supposed virtuous veneer lies the most devious devils devising horrid schemes of hotel debauchery and a wake of flaunting inseminations that not even Maury Povich can sort out. These were not the birds you took home to meet mother unless you were looking for a new sister or brother. Harv, the toucan with a heavy heart, pondered that he might have to do the right thing. As soon as he let go conniving his way to a fortune, an epiphany came upon him on how to secure a legitimate bankroll. He would start a TV show called BND, Birds' Naked Derrieres, and he would expose the charlatans for what they were and be applauded... Or ridiculed... For being a gossip cock louder and earlier than any rooster in the land.

Before the world could be infected with the stolen sound perpetrated by the Mocks of Sin, Harv's first episode stole their thunder before they shot any lightning. He revealed the source of their song and Ed's song was none other than the ostracized duo, Harold and Malena. The world refused to believe this at first, until the audio experts broke down the songs and compared it to what Harold and Malena had sung during the competition. It was a perfect match. A beckoning arose from the masses for Harold and Malena to return and sing songs again for the world to enjoy. A few though, declined to welcome them back saying if Harold still sings as a Swallow while being a Sparrow and Malena still sings as a Sparrow while being a Swallow, we cannot allow such malfeasance to influence the youth to do even more vacuous acts of dishonesty. They were quickly told, "Get over yourself! The only ones who are being dishonest here are those amongst the Sparrows and Swallows who simply refuse to admit that the greatest voice they ever heard sung in their own tongue was done *by their rival."*

A dule of doves and a charm of hummingbirds were sent to offer an emancipation proclamation for Harold and Malena to rejoin the kingdom of birds again as honored troubadours for life. Harold and Malena thanked the doves and hummingbirds for coming all this way to share with them what they considered to be good news. Aloe, one of the doves, asked Harold and Malena, "Aren't you coming back with us to sing your songs to the world now that the world has opened itself to you?"

Malena spoke first, "If we give to the world only what the world wants, the world will not grow up and mature and take care of what the world needs."

Ryan McSoiledbottoms, a Scottish hummingbird, who claims to be on speaking terms with the Loch Ness monster, said, "We don't understand."

Harold calmly replied, "the world wanted us to go away, so we went away. Now the world wants us to come back, but the world forgot to ask us if we want to come back."

Tori, another dove, "I guess they figured asking would have been a formality."

Malena snapped back, "Or a courtesy."

Remy, another hummingbird, much quicker mentally than the rest of the diplomatic party cut to the chase, "What are your demands?"

Harold and Malena spoke in synch, "We have no demands except one." They turned and looked at each other and laughed at how many times they had practiced that response without ever thinking they would actually say it.

Malena then continued, "You return and tell those dimwits and nincompoops that you call your leaders, that if they want us to truly return and sing our songs for the world to enjoy, then they must do one thing and one thing only."

*She then gave the floor to Harold.
"The competition must come to an end."*

The doves and hummingbirds fluttered about in frenzied agitation. For no one had ever challenged the sanctity of the competition. Without any further explanation, Malena and Harold flew away leaving the doves and hummingbirds helpless with a message that no one expected them to bring home.

*The disappointment and utter melancholy which swept through the kingdom when Harold and Malena were not seen returning with the doves and hummingbirds alarmed even the most stable of governing bodies. The worst was anticipated.
"Please don't tell us that they've passed on."*

One of the doves replied, "We won't tell you that."

"You won't tell us because it's too hard to tell us?"

One of the hummingbirds spoke, "No, we won't tell you because they are very much alive but the message they want us to deliver to you will be received even less graciously than if we had told you that they had passed on."

"So they're alive but refuse to return?"

"It's not that they refuse to return, it's just that when they do return, they refuse to do so to this world as it is."

A commotion of misunderstanding, ignorance, bias, prejudice and every other misconception in between quickly spread throughout the kingdom. Every single leader was asked, "Can you bring back Harold and Malena to sing the most beautiful songs to us in the most beautiful voices?" Every single leader would shrug their shoulders and rationalize that it was not up to them to bring Harold and Malena back, it was up to Harold and Malena to grow up, and succumb to the will of the people and return.

Each leader who gave this answer was soon written off as impotent and a speaker of the most dreaded lie of all. The lie of knowing what had to be done to secure a result, but avoiding it being done because to have it done would end their political careers.

The people knew that Harold and Malena would return if the leaders would abolish the competition. The leaders rebutted. "No two birds, no matter how glorious their voice and song, are worth ending the very event which provides our status as songbirds among the kingdoms of birds." In other words, the leaders who use the competition to control the creative output of the birds would lose control if the competition was abolished.

The mob argued the competition is not being brought down for those two. The competition is being brought down for all of us. The leaders secretly agreed that the competition would be brought down for everyone and not just those two but did not agree that the competition should be brought down.

What then happened was the same ole same ole, the many riled up at the few but unable to do more than complain and vent that they could do nothing about the few who could do anything to them; therefore, the competition continued and Harold and Malena remained far away.

When news reached Harold and Malena that the leaders of the competition did not give in to their demands of ending the competition so that they would return to sing to the masses, Malena said to Harold, "We have no other choice but to enter the competition and win it like no one else has ever won it."

Harold smiled and said, "Let Project Competition Cacophony be underway."
Word spread fast that Harold and Malena would reenter the competition. The leaders of the competition felt at ease because they could control the results and therefore, for the most part negate and nullify Harold and Malena's influence upon the masses.

The masses, titillated by the return of Harold and Malena, didn't care if such meant that the competition would only be reinforced that much stronger with the appearance of Harold and Malena in it. All the masses cared about was that Harold and Malena would sing to them with an original song one more time.

Harold and Malena agreed with the judges to open the show. Typically, the show opener merely warmed up the crowd, to get the show underway, and had no shot to win. Harold and Malena recognized that the judges were letting them know they were not going to allow them to win this competition by scheduling them to open the show. Of course, Harold and Malena had expected and fully embraced this underhanded move by the judges. They had an underhanded surprise of their own for the judges.

Harold and Malena used their prep time for the show to meet and greet with as many fans and fellow contestants as time would permit. Rather than be holed up in a private room, nitpicking and squabbling over every nuance and minutiae of the performance, they felt it more important to share their personal vibe one on one with those who were old friends and those becoming new ones.

The commentators were commenting about the placement of Harold and Malena to open the show. "No one has ever won as *the show opener. But perhaps Harold and Malena are not interested in winning, that they just feel good to be back on stage again singing before the masses."*

Another commentator said, *"I spoke to them, as they were warming up, and they were determined they were going to win. No, actually, they said* **we** *were going to win?!"*

The other commentator picked up that thought and professionally carried it over for the audience to understand. *"Well yes, of course, we're all going to win, just to have them back singing for us."*

When Harold and Malena walked on to the stage and were introduced, the applause was deafening. The commentators commented, *"It's so loud in here I can't hear myself!"*

Seeing the other commentator's beak move one of them asked, *"What did you say?!"*
But got no response due to the roar of the crowd.

Malena hushed the crowd by gracefully raising her wings and lowering them as the volume of appreciation subsided. Harold then raised his wings and slowly brought them down until the quiet became deafening. No one in the audience was moving, not even the commentators, as they anticipated this moment that none of them would ever forget. Only one judge tapped one claw on a table, which brought a cold stare from Harold and Malena and everyone in the audience until he stopped.

Harold began, *"Thank you for your stilled silence. Such is required for our song to be heard where it is meant to be heard."*

Malena, *"Yes, most songs are meant to be heard by the body so that we can dance along with the music of life. This song though, was meant to be heard by your heart so that you can sing along* with us as we celebrate life."

Harold, "It's not that we wrote this song so that we could sing it to you. We wrote this song for you so that you could sing it to us."

The judges shifted uneasily in their seats at what they were hearing.

Harold continued, "For what good is a song that doesn't move us to sing along? What good is a singer that doesn't inspire you to sing your own song?"

Malena, "We know it is forbidden during the competition for the audience to participate while the contestants perform, but we know why we are the opening act, and since we're not going to be allowed to win the competition, we ask you to join in and sing with us our song even though it's forbidden."

The judges would normally disqualify anyone on the spot for showing such open defiance toward them in the competition, yet, since Malena and Harold had already accepted they would not be allowed to win, they would allow this little exhibition of defiance to continue.

The crowd murmured excitement alongside confusion so Malena took hold of the reigns. "You're asking yourself, how can you possibly sing along to a song that you've never heard before? Yet I tell you, this is the only song you ever really heard in your heart when anyone else tried to sing any song. For, why is it that we sing at all? Is it because we love music? Is it because nothing pleases us like music does?"

Harold chimed in, "Is it because we are birds, and this is what birds are expected to do? Yes of course, it is all this and yet more."

Malena, "Much more. We sing rather than just talk to show the harmony between what is in our hearts and what we think in our minds and feel in our souls. No other expression can show this harmony as well as singing does."

Harold, "So why do we sing songs which produce disharmony and discord between us? Why do we use our most important gift against ourselves and for what?... To create a world whereby competition dictates to us what is a quality song of intrusive exclusion rather than songs of encompassing inclusion? We do this because we do not know any better. No one has ever sung to us from this place until tonight."

Malena, "As you know, we were exiled for not being able to sing in the voice of our ancestors, yet what we discovered in the wilderness of obscurity, is that the song does not care whose voice sings it. The song only cares to be sung. Yes, it is not that we are returning to sing you a song, we are here to share a song that is shared with all of us no matter where we are in the world or how we're treated by anyone."

Even though Harold and Malena were just talking, it felt like they were singing within the heart of those in the audience.

Malena, "For where can you go that your heart is not already there with you?"

Harold, "And how may you respond and react to what others do to you when knowing no matter what you can always show love?"

Even the judges felt a stirring within.

Harold and Malena then turned to look at each other as would the audience when they sang this song.

Harold instructed those in the audience to turn and look the bird next to them in the eyes and heart to heart rather than gaze up at them as they sang the song. Malena instructed those watching on TV to do the same because she added, "It is much more important that you share this song, rather than watch this song."

Harold then asked, "Is everyone looking at someone?" And the crowd hollered back a huge YES.

Malena noticed there were a few holdouts. "Judges, that includes you also. No need to watch us, when you're not going to let us win anyway. You didn't stop being a fellow bird when you became a judge."

To the surprise of everyone the judges complied. Harold and Malena took a deep breath which was echoed by many deep breaths in the audience. For a split second, Harold reminisced on the journey that he and Malena had taken to get to this spot. All the many days and nights of hard training under the tutelage of his teacher, Diana, enduring the many smaller shows in competitions that few attended only to fall victim to the bizarre of being unable to sing in his own voice... And then be exiled with the very one who had stolen his voice, as much as he had stolen hers... And the many endless days and nights in the wasteland planning and scheming a masterful return that had more chances of not ever happening, than the one chance it now actually is...

Malena felt no need to look back. She focused only on the future and what this would mean when what they were about to do worked even better than they could imagine. She smiled at Harold, and gave him a wink to let him know it was time to begin. Harold's eyes widened just a tad, and he began the song.

A Capella, as if Harold challenged any music to match the beauty of the voice he knew belonged to Malena, Malena chimed in to sing Harold's part in the song with the same gusto and bravado that he would sing in any song. They repeated the verse again.

And then again. And as they did it for a fourth time, the audience caught on and just two bars behind sang the same verse. The audience knew then, how to participate in the song. Then the music kicked in and nothing would ever be the same again. As Harold and Malena sang with the audience singing just two bars behind, two other contestants, a finch and a lark, joined Harold and Malena on the stage. They began singing the same verse two bars behind the audience.

The judges, even though they were enjoying the harmonized echoing of the audience following Harold and Malena's lead which led to the lark and finch following the lead of the audience, the moment that the lark and the finch crashed the performance of Harold and Malena, they disqualified themselves from the competition. "Serves them right," said one judge to another. "Rules are rules, and if we don't enforce them there will only be chaos." The other judge was actually too busy singing to bother with such trivialities during a moment of greatness.

Soon after, a pelican and a stork, even a blackbird and a robin, alongside an eagle and a wren came onstage and jumped in two bars behind the finch and the lark. The obstinate judge wrote down six more DQs. Soon every contestant joined Harold and Malena singing onstage, always two bars behind the birds ahead of them. There were oogles, there were chickadees, bristlebirds and honeyeaters, logrunners and tit berrypeckers, longbills and babblers, wattle-eyes and whipbirds, butcherbirds and magpies, rockjumpers and ifritabirds, yellow fly-catchers and streaked scrub-warblers, treecreepers and nuthatches, bananaquits and whydahs, gnatcatchers and fairy-bluebirds, flowerpeckers and wagtails, grackles and cowbirds, and many more too numerous to be listed here, all joining in.

The intense wave of emotion that hit each bird group when they heard this song sung in their own language, moved them to transform themselves into a brotherhood of global peace.

Furious, the one and only judge not taken in by this obvious spectacle of subversive competitive sabotage broke free from the spell singing the song had on everyone else, and rushed over to inform the head judge that all the other contestants had disqualified themselves from winning the competition. This meant there could only be two winners. The very two that the judges were determined not to let win no matter what.

The head judge thanked the rule informer for his diligent work, "We can't and must not let that happen."

The rule informer judge smiled, "We must surely not, rules were not made to be broken, rules were meant to be enforced."

The head judge then proceeded to do something unprecedented in the competition, and walked up on stage and joined in singing with Harold and Malena and the rest of the contestants.

The singing continued for what seemed like and hour, but when the tape was reviewed, it was just 24 minutes.

Everyone was now singing along with Harold and Malena at the end and here is a sample of what they were singing:

Here I am singing my song with you singing your song singing a song that had not been sung until we sang our songs together as one. The best songs that any of us ever sing are songs full of hope, full of love, and plenty of merry-go-rounding. Here we are singing as one, singing as we've never sung before. Who dare tell us now that we can't sing in peace and force us to live behind closed doors? We sing this song so you'll sing along to sing your song all day long. All Day Long. All Day Long. Sing Along. Sing Along. All Day Long.

When the last note was sung, everyone bowed and applauded each other. Even though Harold and Malena had been successful in their aim to have the world sing as one, throughout the many different voices it would still come down to the judges' judgment on what it meant within the confines of the competition. Harold handed the head judge his microphone. Loud boos shook the auditorium. Malena scolded them, "Have we learned nothing of ourselves in the unification through that round? Let the head judge speak his piece in peace so that we may show we will never be as they were to us." The crowd hushed at Malena's request.

The head judge announced, "The rules clearly state that any contestant who interrupts a performance in any manner whatsoever is to be instantly disqualified, which means that the only two contestants left to win the competition are Harold and Malena." The crowd erupted in a large cheer.

Harold and Malena had expected this very moment and yet, when the head judge told them to take a bow, Harold retook his mic and surprised all, including the head judge with this proclamation, "Yes, it is true, that every contestant who interrupts us in any manner whatsoever will be disqualified from the competition, therefore not allowed to win. And yes, that does mean, that Malena and I are the only two left to win the competition. And we would accept that victory if the head judge had not overlooked one tiny, small, important detail. Not one of these contestants actually interrupted us. We asked them to join with us in singing this song, which even the judges themselves joined us onstage. Therefore, we all won... Including the judges' group... Which means that every group is now free to sing their own original songs forevermore."

Rex Arumpus, the judge stickler for all rules and legalities rushed the stage to the dismay of all. "It says right here that any contestant who connives a way to ensure their own victory is disqualified even more than those who interrupt a performance.

Therefore, Harold and Malena cannot win, they are just pulling a new stunt because that is all they do is pull stunts. Are we going to let them succeed in making us look like fools? It clearly states in the rulebook that there is a tie among all the other birds and we will employ tie-breaker number six to determine the tie-winner."

It appeared that everything Malena and Harold had planned would to come to no avail.

Before Harold and Malena and the head judge could refute this outlandish ruling, the swift stepped up and said, "If anyone knows about being interrupted while being on stage, it is most certainly me. We all remember when a certain trush bird, a well-known disrupter, decided that I wasn't good enough to deserve honorable mention for participating in this competition for the tenth year in a row, and he showed he had more ass than melody. And I declare, that if Harold and Malena aren't considered the winners, then none of us are winners. That's not to say we're losers, because we know who the real loser is, right Rex Arumpus?"

The head judge took control of the proceedings. "Alice the swift is correct. Rules are meant to be used as a way to measure what is right and what is wrong. Rules are not commandments that make us do what is wrong and pretend that it is right, which would be the case here."

Rex Arumpus interjected, *"But the rules were put in place to keep us from being tempted to do what is wrong, therefore one either follows the rules and keeps the competition untarnished or one abandons or breaks the rules and taints the entire competition."*

The head judge, who by the way is named Simon said, "Take a look at who you see on this stage. Do any of us appear as followers? No, we are the leaders of the new song that shall be sung throughout the kingdom. We don't need a rule to dictate to us what we know is right in our hearts, and what is right in our hearts is a new way to sing together as one."

Security, handled by the condors, swooped in and removed Rex Arumpus from the building.

Malena added, "That's right, the competition served a purpose: to focus us on the importance of the song in relation to the singer. Tonight we experienced the importance of the song in relation to us singing as one."

Harold added, "Yes, keep in mind as you sing, it is one thing to sing of peace, yet quite another to sing of peace peacefully."

Malena expounded, "Through the competition we sought to uplift one bird and then a group of birds, over the rest. And for what purpose? To keep alive the same avenues and channels of hate and envy from our ancestors alive and well during our time?"

Harold then added, "More importantly, is that you learn the origin of music through this song--"

Before Harold could finish his statement, Jane Outorout, the host of the event, a pink flamingo with a very suspicious background who once released a song titled "Yell (Your Azz Off If You Wanna Sound Like a Champion)," interrupted due to a hard commercial break. "We'll be right back after these important messages." Jane Outorout then turned to an angry Harold, "You will not be allowed to reveal the origin of music during this broadcast. So please, stick to the music, not the subversive philosophy. When we return from the break, we will return to a reprise of your song and then sing out through the credits. Got it?"

Harold, anticipating such a move, kept feigning anger and begrudgingly agreed. He and Malena had decided when this happened, they would then alter the lyrics enough to reveal the secret anyway. By the time they sang the new lyrics, it would be too late to censor them. This plan appeared foolproof except for being censored was the least of Harold and Malena's worries. A certain Raven, who had once cast a spell upon Harold so he would sing like Malena and Malena so she would sing like Harold, had snuck onto the stage. For she was far from done casting spells and making sure she remained the only one who could use the power of the secret of the origin of music. So when programming returned, and Jane Outorout reintroduced Harold and Malena to those watching, the raven cast her largest spell to date. When Harold and Malena began to sing, they could suddenly sing in their own voice. To the surprise of everyone, especially Harold and Malena. Yet, when the audience joined in, it sounded the same, but no one in the audience sang in their original voice. At first no one noticed. Until the lark and the finch began to sing, and the lark sang like the finch and the finch sang like the lark. All larks and finches throughout the world quickly realized, they sang as the other had sung. All the larks and finches then stopped singing, and began blaming this treachery on Harold and Malena. For if they had not begun to sing this song, they would not have experienced the same fate that had once befallen Harold and Malena. They stopped paying attention to the meaning of the song, which was to reveal the origin of music, and their iron hatred began to grow toward Harold and Malena, who now sang in their original voices. What sorcery had Harold and Malena inflicted upon them? The same thing happened with the pelicans and the storks, the blackbirds and the robins, and the eagles and the wrens. Until there was no group of birds who sang in their original voices. Not even the Swallows and the Sparrows sang in their own voice, except for Harold and Malena. Not one bird heard the message on the origin of music. They were too busy listening to themselves sing like someone else, and panicking if anyone could fix this travesty. Quickly, it was concluded that no one could fix it... That Harold and Malena were nothing more than charlatans who had greatly deceived the world to sing a false song, which is now banned as heresy, so that they could get their own voices back in exchange for everyone losing their voice. Harold and Malena were arrested, put on trial, convicted of sorcery, and sentenced to execution.

Compounding the dire circumstance in which Harold and Malena found themselves were the unsuccessful attempts by the birds to regain their own voices. Now the larks not only sounded like the finches and the finches not only sounded like the larks, every individual lark and finch sounded like a different species of bird, now causing mass confusion within their own group. The more the birds attempted to reverse the curse, the worse the curse became for them. As Harold and Malena's execution date approached, Harv, executive producer of BND, was delivered a package with a message, WATCH THIS IF YOU DARE. When Harv watched the video, he was shocked more than he had ever been shocked, which for Harv, in his line of smut exhibitionism, was quite shocking. On the tape was audience footage of the last competition (for there were no more competitions after the curse), of a certain raven, offstage performing bitchcraft. Harv, who was sick and tired of garbling like a drunk ostrich for his show, wanted to strangle that raven, but he knew two things; one, he would be joining Harold and Malena in the execution line, and two, such would not reverse the curse. So, he set out to find a way to reverse the curse.

What he found out was more dismaying and more disappointing than the dropping ratings and ad revenue for his show. Apparently, once a raven casts a spell, that spell takes on a life of its own. If the raven has cast the spell in such a way that she or he is no longer connected to its nexus, there can be no reversal, the spell is forever. This is why the attempts by the birds to undo the curse have failed. The spell has merely mutated itself against the onslaught of its own demise. You can't blame a curse for wanting to keep on cursing.

Three days before Harold and Malena would be no more, Harv had something happen to him that had never happened before, he had an original idea. What if the solution was not in reversing the curse, but in luring and using the curse to enhance their state of being to a greater height? What if the curse was actually revealing how sick the birds were and how much they were in need of a real cure? The solution to every curse is to find the cure within it. Curing a Curse is the only way, and only Harold and Malena can cure this curse since they were the original targets. Harv knew he must get to them before it was too late, because once they were gone, the curse would be forevermore. When Harv showed the tape to Harold and Malena, Harold was puzzled, but Malena gasped with recognition.

"I know that bitch!"

Harold asked, "You know that bitch?!"

Harv chimed in, "No doubt, she's a bitch."

Malena explained, "Yeah, that bitch has been after my family even before I pecked through my shell. She was in love with my father, even though my father is a Swallow and she is nothing more than a dirty, skanky, stinky raven bitch."

Harold stunned, "I thought my back-story was sketchy."

Harv, titillated, "More, more, tell me more about this raven bitch and your father."

Malena continued, "Now, I'm not going to say that my father and that bitch didn't have a thing. Because she sure acts like my father plugged her. But unlike the rest of us, who can move on when we realize we've made a mistake in a mate, she obviously hasn't let go."

Harold cut to the point, "Why are you showing us this video? In three days time we will be executed for a crime that we obviously did not commit."

Showing us how innocent we already know we are, is like adding emotional torture to an already absurd circumstance.

Harv countered, "I'll show you the videotape to determine if there is anything that you two can do about the curse. If there is nothing you two can do about the curse, setting you free and executing the raven in your place, doesn't get us anywhere past the curse. We just exchange two villains for one."

Malena countered, "So what you're saying to us is this, if we can do nothing about the curse then our innocence and lives don't truly matter."

Harv concurred, "None of our lives truly matter."

Harold stoically, "Alright, fair enough. This is the deal. You take this video to the president and ask him to grant us a Stay of Execution, not a Pardon. Malena and I need some time to figure this out. If we cannot figure this out in thirty days then we will accept our fate."

Malena objected, "Why will we accept our fate if we are innocent?"

Harold sighed, "Malena, we are not fully innocent. You and I will still be blamed because even though the raven is responsible for the curse, there would have been no curse levied if it had not been for your father. Therefore--"

Malena interrupted, "That's not fair. That's not even guilty by association. That is guilty by victimhood."

Harold sighed again, "Malena, being famous or infamous is never fair. We are subject always to their irrational and illogical whimsical opinions on who and what they think we are. We both know they don't really know us. Our only chance, our only salvation, is to figure out how to undo the curse."

Malena nodded.

Harv went to see the president, otherwise known as the chief resident because he proclaimed he wouldn't be leaving office, and showed him the tape.

The president incredulously asked, "What am I supposed to do with this information that I never wanted to be held accountable for ever viewing? Now I have no plausible deniability thanks to your meddling in affairs that you have no business or security clearance in messing up. Is this your only copy?"

Harv, distressed by what he heard, "Yes."

Both knew Harv was lying.

The president, an albatross, "Regardless, if you release this tape now, I will have my team of experts prove to the masses that this is nothing more than a fake, and you are trying to drum up empty sympathy for Harold and Malena. I will then arrest you and imprison you for life. There will be no Stay of Execution. There will be no Pardon. There will be the most watched television event ever, when those two charlatans are executed." Even though the message isn't funny, it sounded funny to Harv, because the president gobbled like a Turkey when he said it.

A second miracle happened to Harv. He actually felt worse for Harold and Malena and their fate than he did over the loss of sensational airtime when he would show the video of the raven casting the spell. Six birds knew the truth: Harv, Harold, Malena, the bird who shot the video, the president and the raven. Everyone else believed in a falsehood. So Harv decided to do the unthinkable. He would confront the raven.

Of course, the instant she scoffed at him, and his silly concern for Harold and Malena, he felt his last strand of hope snap. The raven mocked him, "I dare you to play that video on your show. Such sorcery is not allowed on the television unless it is watered down and diluted into trinkets and superficial incantations."

Harv countered, "But I have permission from the president himself to show this on TV."

Leary, the raven challenged him. "Oh really, the same president who profits from the wars now going on due to the confusion of the birds, their identity and inability to communicate? I doubt very seriously he would disrupt his flow of power and authority over a couple of songbirds."

Harv defiantly insisted, "You watch, I'm going to make sure the entire world knows what you've done, and I will see to it that you are punished."

She defiantly laughed, "After those two are executed, it won't matter. I'll just become another conspiracy theory for losers, and posers and pretenders to get lost in because the masses will have already swallowed that Harold and Malena are guilty. You will look like a fool preaching to other fools."

Harv left in silence.

When Harv delivered the bad news to Harold and Malena, a third miracle occurred.
Harv wept.
In some circles, such meant he was eligible for sainthood. He left Harold and Malena in the same silence that he had left the raven.

Harold and Malena had two days before they would be plucked and tarred and then lit on fire for the entire world to watch. Harold, attempting to make light of their pending gruesome end, "Malena, you know what I'm really gonna hate about the way they're gonna kill us? It's how the pressure from within our heads will cause our eyes to pop out, which they will then auction off to some museum of the weird so little birdies can pretend to stare us down eye to eye."

Malena angry, "Harold, that is the most asinine, despicable, ludicrous, disgusting, repulsive form of surrender I've ever heard. You should be ashamed of yourself!"

Harold laughed. "Malena, we might as well laugh about it, otherwise one could go insane fretting over the absurdity."

Malena, still not laughing, "Sometimes it's just not funny. Sometimes it's actually just serious."

Harold relented exercising his funny bone, "You're right Malena, but what can we do? The president is determined to see that we are executed for a crime that he now knows that we did not commit. The raven, potentially you're mother, refuses to come clean and absolve us of our misappropriated guilt. And Harv, who has the proof of our innocence can show no one for fear of further cursing by the raven and removed to oblivion by the present administration. In short, what does it matter how much we laugh or how serious we get these last two days?"

Malena in sarcastic frustration, "Oh. So since we have 28 days less to prepare for a possible way out of this, you're going to wave the white flag of surrender?"

Harold, "We needed the thirty days for Harv to leak out the video and produce an underground swell of doubt mixed in with hope that we might not be as guilty as we have been sentenced. Two days is not enough to spark such fury. That is why I didn't even bother to ask Harv to do this for us."

Malena surprised Harold, *"I do agree. Two days is not enough time for that to happen. But you know what two days is enough time to have happen? You and I need to write the greatest song ever, a song so great that the instant they hear it they will forgive us and wish to set us free."*

Harold laughed but sounded serious, *"At least my plan was plausible for the thirty days. There's no way we can write a song in two days to even come close for them to forgive us, much less set us free."*

Malena undeterred, *"Pressure's on big boy. If I can master any other bird's voice and song in a day or less, then surely when the stakes are at their highest we can come through with the greatest song they've ever heard."*

Harold, inquisitively, *"What did you say?"*

Malena reiterated, *"Pressure's on big boy."*

Harold stopped her, *"No no, not your feign attempt at manipulation through phony encouragement. I mean that part about you and learning the other bird voices. You can really do that?"*

Malena confidently, *"Yes, of course!"*

Harold, curious, *"When did you learn to do this?"*

Malena, *"When I was a child. I would watch and listen to the other birds and wondered how they sang the way they did. One day, I met the cutest Oriole, and he would sing to me. He was so impressive in his poise of his song that I found myself inadequate in his presence. So each day, when he came to visit me, I would ask him to sing to me the entire time he was in my presence. He would ask me to sing for him, but I never would. I told him that my voice could not compare to his. Therefore it was better that he sing to me."*

Harold interjected, "You have one of the most lovely voices around, why would you tell him that?"

Malena smiled, "Because one day when he asked me to sing for him, I sang in the most beautiful Oriole voice that he had ever heard. He was so upset at me, and yet so enchanted by me that he didn't know whether to leave or stay. That is when I realized that I could learn to sing, and sing well, in any other bird's voice."

Harold, at the beginning of his epiphany inquired of Malena, "Why is it Malena, that if you have the ability to sing in any other bird's voice, were you so shocked that you sang in a Sparrow's voice at the competition. Did you not learn to sing in our voice beforehand?"

Malena laughed, "Okay, you got me, I wasn't surprised that I was singing in a Sparrow's voice, I was just surprised that I was singing in your voice. I had sung in other Sparrows' voices before."

Harold peeled back another layer of his epiphany, "So, when we were cursed, and I sang in your voice, and you sang in mine, what happened to your original voice?"

Malena, chagrined, "You know, I simply forgot how to sing in my own voice."

Harold epiphanized, "That's it!"

Malena, sensing he was on to something, "That's what?"

"Malena, right now, can you sing in my voice?"

Malena, beginning to realize where he was going, "No, I can't."

Harold expected that answer, "Of course not. You have forgotten how to sing in my voice, just as you forgot how to sing in your own voice during the initial cursing. And yet that does not mean that you could not have been taught how to sing in your own voice again, even while cursed."

Malena asked, "But who would have taught me?"

Harold answered with certainty, "Me, of course. I was singing in your voice. Just as you would have taught me how to sing again in my voice. We just might get out of this Malena."

Malena, excited to hear this asked, "How so?"

Harold responded calmly, "I need to formalize a plan. Right now, we need to write that greatest song, because the pressure is on."

They spent the next two days writing what they thought would be the greatest song ever.

Harold and Malena were putting the final touches on their song when the guards barged in to their cell to announce, "It's Showtime!"

The two hour special had already been on for an hour, filled with woeful stories of birds who had tragically suffered when they lost their original voice. War had replaced music as the most commercial enterprise. Songs that didn't make one feel good for going to war received no airplay.

When Harold and Malena were perched on to the stage, President Albatross stepped up to the podium. "Here... They Are..." He bellowed, as much as any Albatross gobbling like a Turkey could bellow. "Here are the two malcontents who were so devious in their prankster ways that they thought it would be comical to pull a stunt which has led to all of our wars and division. Well tonight, we shall serve them justice. Hot... Burning... Justice."

The crowd in attendance, some on the ground but many, many more in the air, chirped a loud roar of approval. The president continued pontificating, "These two are responsible for every ounce of confusion and derision we have inflicted upon ourselves and each other. Just two days ago, they sent a lowlife scumbucket to try to persuade me to give them an unwarranted Stay of Execution." They crowd chirped a loud boo.

Harv watching in horror, begged to no avail to the president through his TV screen, not to name him.

"Yes, you do know him, the infamous Harv from BND television. They had concocted a strange, but baseless theory, that the ravens were behind the curse. Yes, we all know that mysteriously the ravens were not affected by the curse. Of course, we all know why. Their crackle is so repugnant that when it came time to switch, no host could be found, and therefore, it was even greater punishment upon the ravens that they had to keep their own voice. But, I pardoned Harv for foolishly falling for one last scheme of Harold and Malena."

Harv wiped his brow, but he knew President Albatross was not a bird of his word. He expected a knock of danger on his door at any moment.

The president was not finished filling up to be full of himself. "So tonight we will witness what happens to those who think more of themselves than they do for the welfare of the rest of us. Yet, in spite of our propensity for ugly warfare, when we have an opportunity to show and share mercy we most certainly do. We will allow Harold and Malena to sing one last song, in their own voice. So you might as well enjoy it, because when you think about it, this will be the last time we hear any bird sing in the original voice of that bird. So without further adieu, so we can hurry and get on to the execution, here is Harold and Malena's Swan Song. Too bad they won't be singing as Swans, like those poor Peacocks over there."

Harold and Malena expected boos, but none came. Harold heard the same erie silence that he had heard at that first competition. He thought to himself, 'Why are they being so quiet?' and he gazed upon Malena. She had never looked so beautiful. Each of her feathers glistened and sparkled like diamonds in a strobe light. She looked radiant. 'Of course she did,' thought Harold, they wanted to show that true beauty wasn't in the beautiful, true beauty belonged to those who could destroy the beautiful.

Malena began talking to the audience. "What the president said is true, just not true enough to be truth."

Harold chimed in, "Yes, because of us, the entire world is cursed, that is true. But what isn't true enough about that is what you know or rather what you don't know about curses."

Malena added, "You see, a curse is only a curse if you approach it as a curse. There are other ways to approach a curse."

Harold, sensing the confusion of the crowd, "For instance, each of you here now sings in the voice of another bird group, and that is because you have forgotten. Yes, you heard me, you have forgotten how to sing in your own voice. What do we normally do when we forget or do not know how to do something if we really want to do it?"

Malena, without hesitation, "We learn it."

Harold, triumphantly proclaimed, "Yes, we learn it. We are not here to help you break the curse. We are not here to reverse the curse. We are not here to lift the curse. We are here to demonstrate to you that no matter what you are free to learn. That means, you are free to learn how to sing in your original voice again. By admitting and acknowledging that you forgot how to sing in your own original voice, hence, the curse, you will now approach the curse in a way that will nullify the supposed treachery that the curse laid upon you, and be even greater in knowledge and wisdom of your own voice because you will have learned it, therefore earned it, rather than just use it and be subject to losing it."

Malena triumphantly proclaimed also, "Harold and I will now do what the purveyors of the curse say is impossible for us to do. We will now sing our final song in every other voice but our own. For we have learned just like you can, to sing in any voice. This means that you may execute us, based on this curse, but if you remain cursed after our execution, that is nothing more than you refusing to learn."

Harold and Malena then sang what many still call the greatest song ever.

When Harold and Malena finished their song, President Albatross, who had not heard one chirp of their performance because he was too busy celebrating their demise, mistook the standing ovation for himself. "Yes, yes, yes, simmer down now, settle down. I know... The time... Of execution has come. I can feel your appreciation and gratitude already. But please, quiet down, so we can hear them squeal and holler as we pluck their feathers."

But the crowd refused to comply, and a chant could be heard murmuring from every group of birds. The male birds chanted Malena *while the female birds answered back* Harold. *Back and forth it went... Harold... Malena... Harold... Malena... The feather pluckers hopped on to the stage but instead of heading toward Harold and Malena, they walked over to President Albatross and restrained him. When President Albatross attempted to demand to know what was going on, the feather pluckers gagged him. A large video screen was lowered onto the stage. With the video running of President Albatross talking to Harv of BND. Apparently, when dealing with a video addict, you must always consider that you're being recorded. The audience stood frozen as they watched the president falsely blame and gleefully enjoy the upcoming execution of Harold and Malena. Few noticed joining President Albatross in restraints was the raven in the video that Harv had shown to President Albatross. Harv walked onto the stage with a hero's welcome and spoke to the crowd. "As you can see, there will be an execution of two birds tonight. A male and a female. Just not Harold and Malena. President Albatross could have stopped this charade, and the raven could have not been such a vindictive bitch that she screwed us all over. So I say... Let justice be served! Hot... Burning... Justice."*

Harold, always the kindest of hearts, took the microphone from Harv. "True justice leads to mercy. Burning these two alive tonight will only show that we can be more like them than be like our greater selves. Yes, what President Albatross did by profiteering off the curse, and what the raven did by instituting the curse, are most despicable acts. Yet, if I can show them mercy, one who suffered the direct brunt of their actions, to almost my own painful execution, you can forgive them as well for forcing you to learn how to sing in yours or any other bird's voices, so that you can communicate again in peace with each other."

Malena, spirited in her reply, "Killing these two is nowhere near punishment enough compared to them having to live and see us be as one in peace. For by seeing us live in peace as one, and relearn our own voices means that the amount of their effort to stop this from happening is null and void. Too often, those who use division to separate us forget that we can multiply our knowledge beyond their uninformed obstacles of divisiveness to become one sum again."

Harold laughed, "Truth is fowlkies, you were told a truth about us, but that truth wasn't true enough to be **the** *truth about us."*

Harold and Malena led the world, the bird-world, into the time period known as the great teaching and restitution of all things.

So keep this in mind the next time you listen to a bird sing. That bird learned to sing in that voice in order to maintain peace with the other birds. What is it that you are learning about your own voice to maintain peace with others?

Epilogue

Even though Harold and Malena had shown the world that singing and music was better than words, and being able to sing and perform music from any species of birds, still the world had yet to learn one great secret: The Origin of Music. Harold and Malena realized that without the knowledge of the Origin of Music acknowledged globally, any and all birds were still susceptible to curses and false divisions based on lesser versions of themselves. Yet, due to the success of showing the birds they could live and learn in a joyful harmony even while cursed, the birds were now too busy learning how to think, sing and be like the other birds, than to delve deeper into the meaning of why they sang.

Harold and Malena were unable to impart the Origin of Music beyond a few acolytes. They wrote a book which only a few have read to this present day, titled, The Origin of Music is not an Origin nor Music, with a dedication written by Harold:

'To those birds who have mastered how to sing a nd be like any other bird without knowing the Origin of Music, until you know the Origin of Music, you're doing nothing more than walking in the wind. Read this book and you shall soar like no other birds before.'

Many, many years later, long after the arrival of humans banging and twanging their music, after the arrival of animals howling and roaring, after the arrival of frogs croaking, after the arrival of bugs chirping and clicking, so long after anyone could remember, a certain bird, a seagull, asked what many had forgotten to ask, what is the origin of music, and more importantly, why is it I am asking now?

That story, like Adah and the Nine Cats of the Golden Order, is currently unfolding in the sequel to this book.

God Declares
As The Devil Tells

God declared, "I am the Truth."

The Devil sighed, "I guess that makes me the lie then."

God declared, "You are the Lie."

The Devil countered, "That's what I said!"

God declared, "Such is not Truth until uttered by God."

The Devil exasperated, retorted, "So, even if I speak the truth, it is a lie until you utter it, how is this so?"

God declared, "You use words to try and reveal Truth, when I use Truth to reveal words... Lying is when one uses words as a concealment for Truth."

The Devil retorted, "So, you say that I don't even reveal any truth in my words even as I use the same words as you do?"

God declared, "Not when you use those words to act like you are me rather than be who you are alongside me."

The Devil asked, "If my purpose is to lie, and you always tell the truth, am I just here so you can tell the truth about lying?"

God declared, "I always do tell the Truth, and you show that I can Lie if I need to."

The Devil quickly responded, "So you ARE saying that I am you."

God declared, "Not unless I say so."

The Devil responded, "This is maddening, you get to tell the truth about what a liar I am, and I get to lie about you and how much of a truth-teller you are. So I end up revealing more truth in my lies than your truth ever reveals about my lies."

God declared, "Not unless I say so, you would be better off telling the Truth that you are a Liar, and that everything you say is a Lie, than trying to Lie that you are telling the Truth about how everything you say is a Lie."

The Devil, exasperated, "That's just the same thing! Either way I'm a liar!"

God declared, "No, in the former you're sincere and genuine and authentic and pure to the nature of your core... In the latter you deserve every name they call you, including the Devil."

So the Devil, resigned, "Sounds like I'm better off either way."

God declared, "You would be better off saying nothing because everything you say is a perversion of what I've already said."

The Devil asked, "So, you are saying that since I am not you, I cannot use words like you, so therefore I would be better off letting you censor me into silence and just listening and reacting to everything you say without sharing my understanding of what you said because no matter what I say will turn your truth into a lie because all I say is a lie unless you say it is not so."

God declared, "If I say you tell the Truth, then you do."

The Devil asked, "Did I just tell the truth?"

God declared, "You did until you asked."

The Devil exclaimed, "You are so seriously mind-fucking me right now!"

God declared, "That is because you haven't accepted and embraced that the power of whether or not your words Lie or tell the Truth does not belong to you, it belongs to me."

The Devil responded, "So you're telling me that I can't tell the truth, I can only declare something as true; and I can't declare something as true until I realize that something's not true without that declaration no matter how truthful I tell it, because I tried to tell it as a truth rather than simply declare it as a truth and let it speak truth to the one listening to me."

God declared, "Only I can declare that which is True or not True."

The Devil asked, "I don't get to declare the truth?"

God declared, "Only God can declare Truth, anything else is you telling the Truth that you can Lie about being able to declare the Truth through only a telling of the Truth, which by the way, I declare as Truth and there is nothing you can say which can declare this otherwise."

The Devil surrendered, "So, I might as well just sit in the corner during your power point presentation of declarations and act like a plant and say nothing at all."

God declared, "Just because you have hidden yourself from yourself does not mean you are actually hiding..."

The Devil laughed, "Coming from the Greatest Hider of All Time, the irony of that declaration is so delicious that I needn't have dessert for an eon and my sweet tail will still be satisfied."

God declared, "I only appear hidden because those who declare to reveal me try to do so without being me; and I only appear to hide because those claiming to have found me while not being me are actually trying to hide me from anyone else being me because I do not hide from myself."

The Devil queried, "So, I can't declare as you until you declare I am you?"

God declared, *"No, until I declare you are me."*

The Devil asked, *"What's the difference?"*

God declared, *"Trying to act like you are declaring what I have already declared is the root of all your Lies."*

The Devil responded, *"So I can't declare what you have already declared?"*

God declared, *"I have no need to repeat myself."*

For the first time in their exchange, the Devil remained silent.

God declared, "Because one can't reveal what is not hidden... The Truth is never hidden. You cannot reveal what has already been shown, you will only conceal it again and then make it appear you can reveal it in another concealment over and over and over again."

The Devil chagrined, "How will I ever communicate properly with others if everything I say is a lie that may or may not be true, depending on your declarations?"

God declared, "I have a way for the Truth and the Lie to dwell in harmony."

Incredulously, the Devil requested *"Enlighten me."*

God declared, "Here, let me introduce you to Adam and Eve."

The Devil for the first time in a long time, gave God the kudos that God deserves and felt a tiny bit of joy in knowing that he need not declare what God has already declared.

For a short time anyway, that is, until he introduced himself...

---written on 6-16-16

On The Authors

While the world is fast learning to communicate in one language,
and the time of a new Nimrod fast approaches,
Diana is fully learning to be fluent in all the languages
because Diana knows what matters most is
not in speaking one language, but speaking from
one understanding in any language.

"Confusion
no matter how well
it's communicated is still confusion.
Truth,
no matter how poorly communicated,
can still be felt as truth."

Damon is the actor who
portrays the Magic Mountain Man
in the Movie,
Holy Galileo!
Adrien Brody swears Damon is the actual
Magic Mountain Man,
but, Adrien is an actor and the World knows
that no actor can be trusted!

See more at

damonwhite.com

Nostraamus, prediction for 2016,"A great revolt will end taxation forever. People refuse to pay the tax to the king. On that day, many will celebrate freedom in a country that taxes mercilessly."

The Ramifications of Freedom

The significance of something is not to bring one's focus to that something, for significance is what we call an important sign in order to focus or refocus on what is actually important. How one interprets the sign determines the level of significance of that sign. For instance, read this aloud, 'The significance of being able to read is not to read about reading, the significance about being able to read is to read so that you read to find the significance of what you're reading.' When you said this aloud did you say read (reed) every time or did you slip in a (red) for one of the reads(reeds). More than likely you said read (reed) every time, yet, the fifth read(reed) could actually be a read (red) and be significantly different to one who read it that way. You are free to read this either way, and free to decide which is the correct way, and free to debate for or against either, yet, and this is how the ramifications of freedom come into play, being free to do all this is not the same as understanding and comprehending what just occurred here.

To see more of Damon's Artwork,
*for purchase or observation,
learn more of his philosophy,
and be notified of events associated
with him and his work, please visit:*

damonwhite.com

Damon and Diana welcome all feedback.

*Feel free to contact them through Twitter
@HolyGalileo*

Publisher's Note

DesChamps World Media, through the publishing imprint of DesChamps Books, is proud to bring to the world
Adah and the Great Seven
the eighth in a series of uniquely

intellectual, spiritual and provocative writings

by author Damon M. White,

In collaboration with Diana S. DesChamps.

www.damonwhite.com

Our goal is to present titles with allure and purpose, meaning and depth, applicability and character, while being
entertaining and illustrious. We also enjoy publishing books of appreciation and biography for prominent athletes, musicians and world figures.

For more information from our publishing imprint,

DesChamps Books and/or other projects from DesChamps World Media, please contact us at:

DesChamps World Media

P.O. Box 1292,

Dripping Springs, TX 78620

www.dcworldmedia.com

Tyrannical Peer Pressure

The tyrant or dictator forces people to think they need a tyrant or dictator (so that they think and act based on the idea that the tyrant or dictator thinks should be how people think and act). The people must be forced to obey because it wasn't their idea to have the tyrant or dictator be their tyrant or dictator.

Last Words...

Before truth is intention, one can tell the truth yet intend to deceive and conceal which turns any truth into a lie, one is being truthful but not true. One can tell a lie, yet intend to reveal and enlighten, which turns any lie into a truth. One is being true, but not truthful. One can also tell a lie with the intention to deceive and conceal. One is neither truthful nor true but pure and harmonious with the intention of their content. One is being truthful yet not true. One believes their intention is greater than truth. One believes the truth is greater than one's intention. Those that lie with the intention to deceive and conceal and those who tell the truth with the intention to reveal and enlighten are equally pure and harmonious with their intention to lie and tell the truth.
These are the four basic intentions for speech.

Interpreting the present into a past lie ensures that the inertia and stagnation of humanity's development continues onward into the future. It is easier to accept and embolden the lie, than accept one deceived oneself into believing the lie, because having a lie to embolden is something more for them than the nothingness that they must face from their own imagination if they accept the truth that they had only been believing a lie. At least if they have a lie, they have something, because the truth of knowing that a lie is a lie starts one with nothing, except their own imagination. Even if the ending of a story is a lie, people would rather believe that than have the continuation of a story be open to their imagination. The lie will tell you that this is the end of the book. But the truth is this book has just begun in your imagination.